Dear Readers,

He's back. Who? Mark Donaldson. Tall, hot and Texan, Mark is the hero in *The Cop Who Stole Christmas*. But some of you may remember that in *Gotcha!* he was Jake Baldwin's partner. Now, when I wrote *Gotcha!* I didn't exactly plan to write Mark's story. He was just a hot single cop who was a bit mysterious. I guess that's all it took to get some readers interested, because the emails rolled in asking when Mark's book was going to be released.

So when I was plotting a new book, I decided poor Mark had been hidden away in the closet of my mind for too long. It was time for him to come out and play. ("Play" being the operative word.) So I took him out, dusted him off, and started poking around in the guy's past to figure out exactly who he was and what deep-seated secrets he was keeping. And I found some doozies, too.

Of course, I had to find the perfect heroine for him to play with, and Savanna, with her own list of issues, came to mind. I also wanted to write a Christmas story, so I set the book in December and Santa showed up on the very first page. Of course, in spite of the fact that he's sort of stealing Savanna's car, the book has all the warmth you'd expect from the holiday season. Add the romance, a murder to solve, tons of laughter, and, well, you've got a Christie Craig book.

I want to give a big thank-you to all my readers. In the future, I'll be pulling some other secondary characters

D1518139

from the closet of my mind and writing their books soon. So stay tuned and check out my website for upcoming releases. Oh, and . . . Happy Holidays!

Love,
Christie

Rave Reviews for Christie Craig!

Gotcha!

"Filled with plenty of action, delightfully quirky characters, a mean villain and a rocky road to romance, Craig's novel is an entertaining tale that holds the interest from the first sentence to the final word."

—RT Book Reviews

"Funny, fast-paced, and full of suspense, Craig's latest will delight her fans as well as fans of Janet Evanovich and Harley Jane Kozak."

—Booklist

Weddings Can Be Murder

"Although the plot is threaded with sassy humor, a lighthearted touch, and misaligned lovers hinting strongly of Shakespeare, a deranged psychopath, a trail of murdered brides, and threats of real danger keep the story on the suspenseful side. Craig's lively story puts a new spin on weddings and will appeal to those who like their lethal tales with a little humor on the side."

—Library Journal

"Once again Craig brings a wonderful story to life with a number of likable and interesting characters. There's a quite decent mystery, a fair amount of suspense and two lovely romances."

—RT Book Reviews

"If you want a sexy that will put a smile on your face, a Christie Craig book is the way to go!"

— Night Owl Romance

Divorced, Desperate and Dating

"This sequel to Craig's *Divorced, Desperate and Delicious* is another delightfully entertaining novel with an intriguing mystery. Peopled with interesting new characters and familiar old ones, it also has its share of animal friends that add a lot of humor and warmth to the story."

— *RT Book Reviews*

"I was simply delighted by this breezy, snappy, good-time story . . . This book is sure to brighten your day."

— Beyond Her Book Blog, *Publishers Weekly*

"Christie Craig has penned a humorous tale that is one part suspense and all parts fun."

— Romance Reviews Today

"Christie Craig is the jewel of my finds when it comes to new authors to add to my favorites list. Her characters draw you in immediately, make you care about them in no time flat, and her humor is to die for."

— The Good, The Bad, and The Unread

Divorced, Desperate and Delicious

"Suspense and romance that keeps you on the edge of your seat . . . until you fall off laughing . . . Christie Craig writes a book you can't put down."

— RITA finalist Gemma Halliday

Books by Christie Craig

Divorced, Desperate and Delicious
Divorced, Desperate and Dating
Divorced, Desperate and Deceived
Murder, Mayhem and Mama
Gotcha!
Weddings Can Be Murder
Shut Up and Kiss Me
Only in Texas
Blame It on Texas
The Cop Who Stole Christmas

For more information: www.Christie-Craig.com

Books by Christie Craig
writing as C. C. Hunter

New York Times Bestselling
Shadow Falls Series (Young Adult)

Turned at Dark (Free download!)
Born at Midnight
Awake at Dawn
Taken at Dusk
Whispers at Moonlight
Saved at Sunrise (Novella)
Chosen at Nightfall

For more information: www.CCHunterBooks.com

I Need You

The pounding started on his door. "Shit." His gripped his cup tighter.

Just because she knocked, didn't mean he had to answer.

The doorbell chimed.

Then he heard her. "I know you're in there. I saw you looking out your window!"

Frowning, he went and opened the door. A gust of 34-degree wind blew in and reminded him all he had on was a pair of boxers.

Her gaze shot to his eyes, then slipped down to his bare chest, and then inched down a bit more, where it lingered around the belly button for an appreciative second, and then shot back up.

His gaze bypassed her blue, beauty-masked face and gooey hair and shot to the V opening of her robe, slipped to the swell of her exposed breast and stayed there.

She clutched her robe tighter to hide the nice view. He didn't do a damn thing to cover up. Let her look. It was all she was going to get from him. All he was going to get from her.

He took a slow sip of his coffee. "Yeah?"

"I need you," she bellowed, sounding breathless.

He choked on the hot liquid.

Good line. It had been too long since a woman told him that, but this was a first. Never had it come from one painted like a smurf.

THE COP
WHO STOLE
CHRISTMAS

Christie Craig

The Cop Who Stole Christmas
Christie Craig
Copyright © 2013 by Christie Craig
Cover design and illustration by RM Brand

ISBN: 978-0-991020-60-7

Acknowledgments

To my agent, Kim Lionetti, who helps me make it happen. To my hubby, who years ago taught me that love deserved a second chance. To my assistants, Shawnna Perigo and Kathleen Adey, for helping me along this publishing path. To friends Susan C. Muller and Betty Hobbs for helping me whip this manuscript into shape. You guys are the greatest.

*Dedicated to my father, Pete Hunt,
from whom I inherited my first-class,
fine-tuned art of bullshitting.
It helps writing fiction.
Love you, Daddy.*

Chapter One

"Get your hand off my bumper!" Savanna Edwards clutched her pink, nubby housecoat to her chest against the frigid December air as she bolted across her yard to her driveway. Cold mud oozed between her toes.

"Did you hear me?" she yelled over the sound of *"Grandma Got Ran Over By a Reindeer"* bellowing out of the wrecker. She came to a sudden stop, her breath catching with shock at the sight of the man hooking up her Honda.

Santa Claus was stealing her car.

"I heard you, lady." Crouched down at her bumper, his long white beard dangled between his knees. He even donned the traditional red suit with the floppy hat sporting a white ball. When he finally looked up, his eyes widened.

The cold snuck beneath her robe, and afraid something might be showing, she tightened the housecoat around her. A chilly gust of wind tossed a heavy strand of mayonnaise-laden hair onto her forehead. That's when she remembered she also had on a neon blue facial mask.

"What do you think you're doing?" She'd heard the clanking while soaking in the tub—her Saturday morning pamper-me ritual. Having just replaced her mailbox after the neighborhood juvenile delinquents had smashed it to smithereens, she'd bolted out of the tub thinking she'd caught the hoodlums red-handed.

It hadn't been delinquents she found, but a wrecker backing up into her driveway behind her car.

Santa stood, his eyes roaming over her. "Just doing my job, Ma'am."

"That's my car."

"Title Mama would argue that fact."

"Title Mama?"

"You give them a title, they loan you money? You pay 'em back, no problem. You don't pay 'em back, you get me."

"I didn't borrow money using the title." Even as she said the words, doubt formed in her gut. Her ex was a certifiable asshole, but he wouldn't have stooped this low, would he?

Oh, hell, who was she kidding? Clint had brought his intern into her house while she'd been at the hospital with her dying mom. He had no stooping limits.

He walked to his truck and pulled out a clip board. "Read it and weep."

Savanna glanced at the papers. There it was—her heart plummeted—her ex-husband's signature on the contract. She really did feel like weeping.

When she looked up, Santa was back to work hooking up her car. "Stop! Please. This is a mistake. I got the car in the divorce. So if someone gave him a loan on it, it was . . . illegal."

The wrecker driver's eyes cut up to her. "I hate it when that happens." He actually sounded sincere.

She felt the skin-firming, pore-reducing mask tighten her face. "Just let me call my ex and get this resolved. Please."

"Sorry," he muttered.

Blinking back the sting of tears, she saw a curtain in the house across the street flutter. Her gaze shot to the neighbor's front door. Was he coming to her rescue? If anyone could help, he could.

After ten seconds of no one walking out, her gaze shot back to Repo Santa. "Look, he got the house, I got the car. It wasn't even fair, but I didn't want the house after . . ."

He stood up again. The Jolly Ol' Soul's knees popped, even though he didn't look that old. "You seem like a nice lady. A little weird maybe." He stared at her face. "Really weird, but I have a job to do. I'm Santa, I give to those who are good and take away from those who are bad."

"I haven't been bad." Her heart pounded. She knew if she didn't calm down she was going to hyperventilate. Or worse, she would fly into a complete rage and start kicking St. Nicholas' ass. She could see the headline now: *Local florist bashes Santa.*

Her gaze cut back to the house across the street. She paid city taxes, the city paid her neighbor. That meant he basically worked for her. Tightening her robe's belt, she high-stepped it across the street hoping to make it before Santa got away with her car.

• • •

Mark Donaldson backed away from the window, and stared at the steaming cup of coffee he held. Santa versus Smurf. Had to be a dream. He took a long swig of coffee, gave the caffeine a second to do its magic, and then looked out again.

He wasn't dreaming.

And now his blue-faced, hot-looking neighbor was hot-footing it across the street. He dropped the curtain. She couldn't be coming over here, could she?

He peeked out again. Yup. She was. The pounding started on his door. "Shit." His gripped his cup tighter.

Just because she knocked, didn't mean he had to answer.

Blowing on the too-hot coffee, he waited for her to leave, hoping she'd assume he wasn't at home, or was still in bed. As the pounding continued, he surmised his neighbor was behind on her car payments and . . .

The doorbell chimed.

Then he heard her. "I know you're in there. I saw you looking out your window!"

Frowning, he went and opened the door. A gust of 34-degree wind blew in and reminded him all he had on was a pair of boxers.

Her gaze shot to his eyes, then slipped down to his bare chest, and then inched down a bit more where it lingered around the belly button for an appreciative second, and then shot back up.

His gaze bypassed her blue face and gooey hair and shot to the V opening of her robe, slipped to the swell of her exposed breast and stayed there.

She clutched her robe tighter to hide the nice view. He didn't do a damn thing to cover up. Let her look. It was all she was going to get from him. All he was going to get from her.

He took a slow sip of his coffee. "Yeah?"

"I need you," she bellowed, sounding breathless.

He choked on the hot liquid.

Good line. It had been too long since a woman told him that, but this was a first. Never had it come from one painted like a smurf. Not that he didn't know that below the mask was a pretty face. And while he wouldn't mind another peek behind the robe, he'd seen and appreciated her body numerous times — from his side of the street, and with her clothes on, of course.

Well, he'd undressed her in his mind on more than one occasion, but that didn't count.

The temptation to cross the street and introduce himself had crossed his mind. But logic had intervened. *'Never get your meat where you get your bread.'* Meaning, don't date anyone at work. And while he didn't work with her, he was sure there was some kind of clever idiom about not sleeping with your neighbor. Maybe, *'Don't shit in your own backyard.'* That would work.

As pretty as she was, that had bad idea written all over it. Not that he'd had any other ideas lately. It had been a long time since . . . His gaze shifted back to the V at her neckline.

Another cold wind blew past her. He relented, and still holding the mug, he crossed his arms over his chest. "What do you need?" He knew damn well what she was going to say. But part of him liked having her on his doorstep — even if it wasn't going to lead anywhere.

She hesitated. "You're a cop."

Yeah, that he was. And a plainclothes cop. So how the hell did she know about that? This was a prime example of why he hadn't gotten to know his neighbors. He didn't want them coming to him with their speeding tickets and crap. He frowned. So she thought he could flash his badge and prevent Santa from impounding her car.

She thought wrong. He wasn't even working for Piperville Police Department. He and his partner had recently transferred from Houston to a smaller precinct, Attalla, where they'd both been hired on as Homicide. They'd gotten bored of chasing robbers, and thought murderers would be more interesting.

"Santa Claus is stealing my car." She pointed across the street.

Maybe she'd been a bad girl. "Are you behind on your payments?"

"I don't owe payments on it." She sighed. "It appears my ex-husband got a loan using the title, but the car belongs to me, so legally, if they take the car, they're stealing it."

He looked across the street then back to her. "Was the car in his name?"

She drew in a deep breath. "It doesn't matter. The courts gave it me."

He frowned. "It matters. I'm sure your lawyer told you to get the legal documents changed over."

She glanced back at Santa hooking up her car. He caught another peek at the opening of the robe. Was she . . . *naked* beneath that thing? Things in his boxers started to twitch. Yup, it had been too long since he'd allowed himself some temporary company. The fact that he always went for the temporary kind was another point to why playing with the neighbor wasn't a good idea.

She turned back to him. "I pay city taxes and you work for the city. You have to stop him."

Right there, that's the reason he didn't get to know his neighbors, so how the hell . . . "I'm a homicide detective. If you had a dead body, I'd be your man. But I don't deal with the car repos. I don't even work for this city."

She inhaled. "Well, there's going to be a dead body if you don't stop him, because I'm either going to kill Santa or I'm killing my ex."

Desperation shined in her blue eyes, eyes that looked brighter due to her blue face. Frowning, he walked over to the sofa and snagged his leather jacket, and slipped it on. "All I can do is check if he has the proper paperwork. If he does, you're on your own."

He was right. She was on her own. As Santa drove off with her silver Honda, Savanna Edwards couldn't have looked unhappier. Or bluer. A couple of tears ran down her blue cheeks. But damn he hated seeing a woman cry, even a smurf woman.

And then *bam*! Just like that, he felt bad. He couldn't have stopped Santa, but damn it. Did he have to be so callous? Christ! Was he turning into his parents? Afraid to feel any empathy for fear someone would use it against him?

It wasn't her fault he'd been in a bad mood for two years. Or that during that time he'd only gotten laid a few times. And none of them had even been particularly good. He opened his mouth to apologize, but she spoke first.

"Thanks for nothing!" She stormed back inside her house, slamming the door in her wake.

He sighed. "Merry Christmas."

• • •

Three hours later, Savanna, parked her rental car in front of Juan's Place, to meet her friends for their bimonthly get-together. She'd almost canceled and spent her Saturday buried in her bed keeping her cat company. But since she'd reneged on going on the girl's annual Vegas trip, Bethany, one of her best friends, had threatened to kidnap her if she didn't show. Bethany, a criminal lawyer, didn't make idle threats.

So here Savanna was, pissy mood and all, about to meet her best buds and send them off on a three-day trip without her. Well, at least two of them were best buds. Bethany and Jennifer had been in her life since junior high. Mandy, an acquaintance of Bethany, had joined the group more recently.

"What are you driving?" Bethany, the only redhead in the group, asked, as Savanna dropped into a chair.

"I don't want to talk about it." Spanish Christmas music blared from above and someone with ADD had strung twinkling lights from every place stringable.

"Okay." Jennifer's shrug sent her brown ponytail bobbing off her shoulders.

"It's not okay," Mandy insisted. "We tell each other everything. I even told you about my new boyfriend's fascination with—"

"And we didn't have to know about that," Bethany said. "Now every time I see him, I get this visual of him . . . doing it."

Savanna swallowed. "If you must know, Santa stole my car."

"Santa?" Mandy asked.

"Yeah." She waved down Leonardo, the waiter.

"Do you mean that metaphorically or literally?" Mandy asked.

"Don't push her," Bethany said. "You see that

forehead wrinkle? When she has that, you don't pry. She'll tell us in her own time. She always does."

Savanna rubbed her forehead. "Is it too early for margaritas?"

"This must be serious," Jennifer said.

Savanna slumped back in her chair. "If I get drunk, will one of you drive me home?"

"Of course we will," Bethany said. "You did it for me when I got my divorce."

"Fine." Savanna motioned at Leonardo again.

He offered her a fluttery wave as if to say he'd be over shortly.

"Okay." Jennifer looked at Mandy, who was now working for a manufacturing business. Mandy, blond and pretty, had cut her hair short to downplay her femininity because of her job. "Finish what you were saying about turtle doves."

Mandy sat up and continued, "Well, each department was asked to choose one of the twelve days of Christmas to decorate our department. Mr. Pancy, my boss, wanted to go with the Nine Ladies Dancing. The guy's such a pervert he considered hiring nine strippers. I argued that the doves would be the best choice. I mean, who doesn't love doves? They are beautiful, make cooing noises, and did you know they're monogamous?"

"Monogamous?" Savanna asked.

"Yeah. Isn't that romantic?" Mandy answered.

"Please," Savanna said. "You can't tell me that there's not a male dove somewhere who thinks he has bigger beak, and isn't strutting his stuff in front of some younger, hot-looking dove and saying, 'Hey baby, come to my nest and let me ruffle your feathers while my wife is off taking care of her sick mama!'"

"So it's about Clint?" Bethany looked back at Mandy. "Told you she'd tell us."

"But I thought you said you didn't love him anymore." Mandy sounded concerned.

"I don't love him!" Savanna snapped. "He used the title of the Honda to get a loan, and didn't pay it. I'm soaking in the tub with my blue mask on when a wrecker driver dressed like Santa pulls up and starts hooking up my car to take it away."

"You didn't get the title turned over to your name after the divorce?" Bethany asked.

Savanna shook her head. "I know I was supposed to. It was on my list to do, but—"

"Don't beat yourself up," Jennifer said. "Grief screws you up." Jennifer who'd lost her mom when she was sixteen was still grief stricken. But then again, Savanna could understand. Losing your mom sucked.

"I can't believe Clint did that!" Bethany seethed.

"I can," Mandy added.

"I told that asshole what would happen if he messed with you again!" Vengeance, the kind she used in the courtroom, tightened Bethany's tone.

Savanna rested her palm on Bethany's hand. "It's not your fault." Because Clint was Bethany's cousin, and the one who'd introduced them, Bethany felt responsible. "I married the jerk. You even warned me."

"Give me the information and I'll look into it," Bethany said. "I swear, I'll chew his ass up one side and down the other in court! He'll pay for this."

Savanna reached into her purse and pulled out the paperwork. "Here's everything Santa gave me."

Bethany looked at the paperwork. "Is the guy's

last name really Claus?" She grabbed her phone and dialed a number. "Mr. Claus," she said," this is Bethany Carver. I'm Savanna Edwards' lawyer. Can you tell me . . ."

"Only five more days till Christmas. " Leonardo popped over to the table. "Have you beautiful bitches decided what you want for Christmas yet?"

"I want a body lift," Jennifer said.

"Your body is tight," Leonardo said.

Mandy huffed. "I want my new boyfriend to stop lighting up his farts."

Bethany, still talking to Santa, held up her hand. All eyes went to Savanna. "I want my ex dead with a ribbon tied around his pecker!" She frowned when she realized she'd said it too loud. Laughter filled the restaurant.

"Sorry." Savanna looked up at the waiter and Bethany moving away from the table. "Can I have a margarita?"

Leonardo chuckled. "Honey, you don't have to explain. I've had more than one guy break my heart, too. Men can be evil creatures. But we still love 'em, don't we?"

Right then, Bethany returned. "Okay, I've officially started working on the case." She frowned. "Unfortunately, I can't promise how long it will take or even if I can get your car back. It's already been turned over to Title Mama."

"What are you going to do about a car?" Jennifer asked.

Savanna let out a gulp of air. "I guess I'll have to use the money from the life insurance."

"She'd want you to use it," Bethany said.

"I know, it's just . . ." Tears filled her eyes. "I'm sorry. It's been over a year, and I should so be over this."

Jennifer leaned closer. "You don't just get over your mom dying. Plus you lost your mom and your marriage the same day. That's a double whammy."

Savanna took a deep breath. "I thought I was over the whole Clint thing and . . ." She shook her head. "I am over him. I don't love him. I'm just mad. And . . . using the money doesn't feel right."

"Have you been to her gravesite and talked to her like I told you to?" Jennifer asked.

"No." Savanna's lips trembled.

Bethany leaned her shoulder into Savanna's. "Your mom had the insurance for ten years. It was to take care of you. You shouldn't feel guilty."

"I know that here," Savanna pointed to her head. "I just don't know it here." She put a hand over her heart.

"Maybe this will help!" the deep, slightly accented voice said. "It's on the house." Juan, the owner of the restaurant, a tall, dark and gorgeous man, set a frozen margarita in front of her. "You know, Savanna, there is nothing I wouldn't do for you." He smiled. "Maybe not kill your ex and tie a ribbon around a certain body part, but I would hire it to be done if you wanted me to."

They all laughed, Savanna included. Juan had asked her out a while back, but Savanna had told him she wasn't ready to date. Sadly, it wasn't altogether true. She was ready, or close to it, just not with him.

"I'd do it for her," Bethany said. "And I'd tie that ribbon in a tight bow!"

"Remind me never to make you mad," Juan said and grinned at Bethany.

They all laughed again and the pressure in Savanna's chest lightened. Nothing like being with her friends. And even knowing a handsome guy was interested made her feel . . . Well, it boosted her ego, but unfortunately her ego was the only part of her the hot Latin guy affected. He was like looking at a piece of calorie-laden dessert with fancy frosting. One that she didn't particularly like all that much. It was pretty to look at it, but didn't tempt her.

When Juan left, Jennifer crossed her hands over her chest. "I think you should come to Vegas with us. Forget about this and let's go have fun."

Savanna shook her head. "I can't. Especially now."

"I told you I'd spot you a loan until you decide to use the money," Bethany said.

"No," Savanna said.

Bethany's gaze shifted to the bar. She leaned in and whispered. "Okay, stay home and go out with Juan. Seriously, I'd date him for his butt alone."

"We'd probably get free food and margaritas," Mandy said.

"He's hot," Jennifer said. "And that voice . . . I could come just listening to him talk."

Savanna spoke low. "I just don't feel the spark."

"Divorce impairs your sparking abilities," Bethany said. "Sometimes it takes being recharged." She glanced back to the bar. "And Juan looks like he has recharging potential."

"Oh, my sparking abilities are working." Savanna sipped her margarita, remembering how good her neighbor had looked. "I went to my neighbor begging for help this morning. You know, the good looking blond, green-eyed cop I told you about. Well, even during a crisis, I was sparking all over the place. The guy answered the door without a shirt on and he looked like he walked off a magazine ad. I thought six packs like his were air brushed. But nope."

"Wait," Mandy said. "He's a cop but he didn't stop Santa from stealing your car?"

"I said he had nice abs, not that he was nice. He looked at the guy's paperwork and didn't do a damn thing."

"In his defense," Bethany said, "he couldn't do anything if the paperwork was in order. But I'm glad you said he was there. If I need a witness that you told the guy it was your car, he'll do just fine."

"I'm not sure he'd testify for me. Really, he was . . . almost a jerk. He could've at least pretended to be sympathetic."

"The good-looking ones are assholes," Mandy said. "Look at Clint."

Savanna frowned. "Please, don't give Clint an easy out. He's not even that good looking."

"I don't think Clint's hot at all," Bethany said.

"That's because he's your cousin," Mandy said. "He's just a good-looking asshole," she said with surprising conviction.

Bethany's phone rang. She looked at her screen. "Hmm, it's Santa again."

"Tell him all I want for Christmas is my car back," Savanna said.

Chapter Two

"What are you doing here?"

Mark looked up from his desk at his partner, Jake Baldwin, propped against the doorjamb. "I could ask you the same question. What? Did Macy already kick your ass out?" His gaze went back to the computer as the information filled the screen. "I told you she was too good for you."

"Only because you wanted her for yourself," Jake shot back.

"If I really wanted her, I'd have taken her," Mark teased then refocused on the screen.

"How's that? I'm better looking than you, and your bank account wouldn't have impressed her."

"And that's why I liked her," Mark muttered in humor, as he continued to read. Besides a couple of outstanding speeding tickets, the cops had gone to the guy's house on a domestic violence call last month. The girlfriend, an Amanda Adams, had refused to press charges.

"I swear, you make being rich sound so hard," Jake said.

"It's being rich *and* so damn good looking that's tough," he said and leaned back in his chair. "Where is your better half?"

"At a baby shower." Jake walked in and leaned against Mark's desk. "I went by your house to see if you wanted to shoot some hoops. When you weren't there I thought I'd come here and catch up on some paperwork."

"You should've called," Mark said.

"I was hoping you had a hot date and I didn't want to interfere." Jake gazed at the computer. "What's this about?"

"Just looking into something for a neighbor."

"Savanna?"

Mark eyed him. "How do you know—?"

"I stopped by your house a couple weeks ago and you weren't there. She was mowing her lawn. We struck up a conversation."

Mark's mind went to the time he'd watched her mow the lawn. It'd been right after they'd both moved in . . . over the summer. She'd been wearing shorts and a bathing suit top. He'd gotten a beer and sat by the window to enjoy the view.

He glanced up at Jake. "You're married."

"I talked to her, I didn't ask her out. I even hinted she should meet you."

Mark frowned. "You told her I'm a cop. You're the reason she came banging on my door!"

"Excuse me for sending a pretty woman your way."

"She's my neighbor," Mark said.

"So?"

"You don't shit in your own backyard."

"What?" Jake laughed.

"It's a comparison. You know, like you don't get your meat the same—"

"Got it. Believe it or not, even without a master's degree, I've heard of idioms, but what I don't get is why you're equating sex with shitting. No wonder you don't get lucky very often. And when you do, they don't hang around."

Mark stared up at his partner having a little more

fun than he should. Not that it was a surprise. Giving each other hell was what they did. "Since when is my getting lucky any of your business?"

"Since you get grumpy when you don't get any." Jake looked back at the screen. "So who's Clint Edwards?"

"Savanna's ex." Mark frowned. "She had her car repoed this morning. She said her ex used the title illegally to get a loan and he hasn't been making payments."

"Sounds like a nice guy."

"Yeah."

"So you and her . . ." He held out his hands. "Are you . . . you know?"

"No, she just came over this morning hoping I'd save her car from Santa."

"Santa?"

Mark frowned. "The wrecker driver was dressed up like Santa."

"Ouch. That would make it sting more."

"Yeah," Mark said.

"So you're going to look into it for her?"

"No, I was just . . ."

"Looking into it."

"Yeah, but she admits that the title was still in her husband's name. I can't do crap."

Jake's brow pinched. "Then why are you even checking?"

"I don't think she was pleased with me when I couldn't stop it."

"Oh, hell, you gave her the Donaldson 'tude, didn't you?"

"I don't have a 'tude." But he knew it was a lie.

Christie Craig

His upbringing had left residuals on his outlook.

"Yeah, you do. You act like a dick. Then you realize your rich brat persona is coming out, and you feel
bad and you go overboard trying to be nice. It's how
you operate." Jake crossed his arms over his chest. "I'll
bet you've already apologized."

Mark frowned. "No." He'd been planning to when
he saw a car rental place pick her up. Then when she'd
driven back home, he'd gone to get dressed, but she'd
left before he'd stepped out.

But there was always tonight.

• • •

The cold had Savanna pulling her coat closer
around herself, but she continued to talk. She wasn't
sure how long she'd been here, an hour, two, long
enough for her butt to go numb, but it felt right. Not
the numb butt, but the talking.

"I know it's crazy, but it feels like if I use the
money I'm saying that I'm okay with you dying. And
it's not okay. I don't want your money, Mom. I want
you. Fifty was too damn young." Savanna brushed the
tears back.

She'd ended up hanging out the entire day and
evening with Bethany and Jennifer. Then Mandy came
over later and Savanna drove them to the airport.

She'd started home after that, but she remembered
Jennifer's question. *Have you been to her gravesite and
talked to her like I told you to?*

She hadn't. Hadn't come back since the funeral.
She blamed it on being busy at the flower shop,
blamed it on having to deal with the divorce. Blamed

it on the fact that the cemetery was an hour and a half away. But tonight the truth clawed at her conscience. She hadn't come because it was easier to pretend it hadn't happened. Sure, she missed her mom like the devil, but missing her wasn't the same as accepting she'd never see her again, that they'd never spend an afternoon drinking tea and talking about their next mother/daughter vacation. She'd never spend an entire day shopping for the craziest Christmas mug, or look forward to seeing what kind of mug her mom would get her.

This next year they were supposed to go to New Orleans, tour the old homes, hit a few casinos, drink café lattés and eat tons of beignets.

There would be no beignets.

So instead of going home, she'd driven to the cemetery. One of the gates had been locked but she found the side gate open. The moon provided just enough light for Savanna to see her way to the back of the tree-laden cemetery. It should have been scary, surrounded by graves and huge trees with Spanish moss dangling from them like in some scary movie. But it wasn't. Maybe because she didn't believe in ghosts, if so her mom would have come back, or maybe because Savanna really wanted to talk to her mom.

So sitting in the cold, dark graveyard, the moon's silvery glow the only light, she told her mom she'd been right about Clint not being the right guy for her. Though she wasn't sure he was anyone's right guy. She told her about Santa stealing her car, and for some reason she told her about the rude, shirtless, great-abs neighbor. As time slid by, she finally told her mom goodbye . . . for the first time. It hurt like hell, she cried. Well, more like she wept. But it was cathartic.

As she got up to call it a night, the moon suddenly got lost behind a cloud. The dark got darker. The wind whispered through the graveyard. And then she heard it. A shuffling noise right behind her. Her heart stopped and she swung around.

Chapter Three

Mark stayed up late catching up on his Netflix. After he showered, he'd headed to bed when he heard a car crank its engine. Wearing nothing but a towel, he went to his bedroom window. His eyes went straight to Savanna Edward's driveway. A pair of taillights rolled past Savanna's house as if they might have just pulled away from her curb, but it wasn't the rental car he'd seen her drive away in earlier.

He went to bed, but for some reason instantly recalled the peek he'd gotten beneath Savanna's housecoat. But damn, he had to stop obsessing over her. He owed her an apology and planned to give her a number to a lawyer he knew accepted pro bono cases. Obviously, if her car being impounded was a big deal, she couldn't afford a lawyer. But after that, he'd retreat back into his cave, and secretly have his fantasies about her.

He didn't need to shit in his own . . . dropping back into bed, he raked a hand over his face. Jake was right. That was a bad comparison, but the point remained. He didn't need to start a relationship with a neighbor. It could get messy. He didn't do messy.

He just walked away. Or they did.

I don't want to be married to a cop. Robyn's words whispered through his head.

He hadn't been thrilled with her career choice of political advisor. It reminded him too much of his parents, whom he'd wanted to escape, but he'd accepted it because he loved her. Who knew the love hadn't been a two-way street?

Your dad told me he's cutting you off if you don't take the bar exam.

His dad always made threats. His mom wouldn't let him carry through with them. But it wouldn't have mattered. Most of the family money didn't come to him through his dad. It was a trust fund from his grandfather, but Robyn hadn't known that. And he hadn't known or realized his money had been so important to her.

Grow up, Mark, stop playing cops and robbers, and do as your dad says. Or . . . I walk away.

Ultimatums, he hated them. So he'd opened the door and gave her directions out of his life. He was better off without her. He knew that. His biggest issue wasn't getting over her. It was getting over feeling like an idiot. Feeling used. They had dated for two years, lived together for six months. He'd loved her. Thought she'd loved him. Thought she was marrying him for himself and not for the family's money or prestige.

After that, every relationship he was in, with the exception of his relationships at work, had him second-guessing people's motives. Even if it wasn't about his money. His last almost girlfriend, who didn't know about his bank account, whom he'd dated for only a couple of weeks, had handed him a stack of parking tickets.

I thought this was one of the perks of dating a cop.

Turning on the television to chase away his thoughts, he watched a reality show about pawn shops. At the commercial, he heard another car pull up. He glanced at the clock, midnight. He shot up to the window. It was her. Alone. What had kept her out all night? A man? Did his neighbor have a lover she'd run to after her bad day? Lucky guy.

He watched her hurry to her front door. He'd bet she was all warm and soft under that jacket. His hands itched to slip under that black cloth and find that warmth, to touch what had peeked out under the housecoat this morning. What kind of lover would Savanna be? A little wild and crazy? Slow and sensual? Right now, both appealed to him.

But damn, he needed to get that woman out of his head.

• • •

As Savanna unlocked her door, the hair stood up on the back of her neck. She'd been jumpy since the skunk startled her at the cemetery. The thing had stood there with yellow beedy eyes and just stared at her. She'd been lucky he hadn't turned around and skunked her.

When her hair continued to dance on her neck, she looked over her shoulder, her gaze ending up at the house across the street. She could swear she saw the blinds shimmy. Was he watching her?

Her mind recreated an image of Mr. Hottie without his shirt—a dusting of light brown hair across his chest, then a treasure trail disappearing into his boxers. Remembering his I-could-care-less demeanor this morning, she shook off the image.

Boots meowed behind the door and Savanna walked in. The darkness enveloped her, reminding her that, besides her mom's cat, she was alone. Completely and totally alone. Her chest suddenly felt hollow.

The heater kicked on and her relatively new one-story house, in a semi-nice neighborhood, groaned. She felt the darkness again. Obviously she'd been so upset in leaving today that she'd forgotten to leave the entryway light on. Had she even fed Boots this morning? She recalled setting out a dish. Okay, she wasn't a totally bad pet owner. "Kitty, Kitty."

She dropped her purse on the small bench seat in her entryway. Boots did a figure eight around her ankles. Savanna knelt to give the cat a scratch behind the ear, her loneliness fading. "Sometimes I wonder if Mom didn't get you for me." Another sting of tears hit her eyes. Her mom had gotten the cat after she'd been diagnosed with cancer and only two months before she died.

"You hungry? Let me change clothes and I'll feed you."

Savanna darted into her bedroom, hit the lamp switch, stripped off all her clothes and donned a white silk nightshirt. The warm slinky fabric caressed her body. In some distant part of her brain, she longed for something other than silk to touch her. Maybe Bethany was right, it was time to start dipping her toe into the dating pool. Her mind went to Juan, then pushed the thought away. Not him. The image of the neighbor's naked torso filled her head.

"Not him either," she muttered, but her skin went super-sensitive again.

She tossed her clothes in the hamper. Boots called her from the other room. "Coming, sweetie."

She walked through the dark living area and into the darker kitchen and headed for the stove to switch on the oven light.

"You hungry? Mama's—" Her foot caught on something and she went down.

"Shit," she muttered, her knees taking the brunt of her fall. Unsure of what had tripped her, she went to stand, and instantly became aware of something sticky on her palms.

Standing up, she rubbed her right knee, and felt more moisture there. Boots meowed again. Savanna looked up, her vision still adjusting to the darkness, only allowed her to make out shapes. Her breath caught when she realized exactly what the shape looked like. She turned and hit the light switch. Light splashed across the room. From that second on everything seemed to happen in slow motion.

She blinked. Her lids fluttered closed, then open.

She saw the dark sticky red substance on her palms—and on her knees. She drew a mouthful of air into her lungs. The metallic smell filled her nose. Not believing her eyes, she swiped her hands on her night shirt. The smear of red on white had her choking on another gulp of air.

She raised her eyes. She saw . . . him.

Clint.

Clint naked on her kitchen floor.

A naked Clint lying too still.

A naked Clint with his eyes open, but with no life.

She saw Clint's throat . . . slashed.

Saw Clint . . . dead.

Blood pooled around his body.

A ribbon tied around. . .

She saw Boots' bloody paws swatting at the ribbon.

She screamed, but nothing came out.

She turned and ran.

Ran for the door.

Ran out the door. Without her keys.

Ran without a thought of where she was going. Or that she didn't have on any underwear.

Then she remembered. *If you had a dead body, I'd be your man.* Her neighbor's words echoed in her head like a dream. The scream locked in her throat finally escaped.

The dark night seemed to swallow it.

She bolted across the street into his yard. She continued to scream. Her mind felt numb as if someone had just given it a shot of Novocain. Clint's image kept flashing in her head.

Black dots filled her vision. She pounded on her neighbor's door, her knees wobbled, the numbness in her mind spreading to her arms and legs.

• • •

Mark had barely got in bed when the scream had him jackknifing up. The pounding at his front door had him grabbing for his gun.

He got almost to his front door when he realized he was naked. Bolting back to the bedroom, the screams had him foregoing get dressed. He snagged his towel and darted back out.

The cry for help grew louder. He ran to the window to see what awaited him on his porch. His neighbor. Just his neighbor—screaming in a frenzy.

He knotted the towel around his waist and opened the door. "What is it?"

His kept his gun down, but his gaze shifted around, seeking a threat.

Nothing. No threat.

He focused back on her.

She'd stopped screaming, her whole body working to bring the oxygen in and out. Shaking. Uncontrollable shaking. Eyes wide. White face.

Panic. He'd seen it numerous times on the job.

But it was what was on her nightshirt that had his breath catching. Blood?

"What happened?" he demanded.

"Body." One word slipped out. She slumped forward, falling into a dead faint.

"Shit!" He barely managed to catch her.

Chapter Four

With his neighbor in his in arms, Mark slammed the door shut with his foot, carried her to his sofa, dropped her down, and hit the light.

His gaze traveled up and down her still body. Blood covered her white nightshirt. His heart raced. He crouched down between the sofa and the coffee table. Unsure how badly she was hurt, he feared the worst.

He pulled up her nightshirt, expecting to find wounds, but found a pale whole body. No bullet holes or knife wounds. Just a . . . he swallowed . . . a perfect, naked, beautiful body.

Remembering how badly head wounds bled, he gently ran a hand over her scalp searching for a wound. Her soft blond hair stirred through his fingers. No wound.

"Savanna?" he called her name. "Wake up."

She didn't stir. Dropping his gun by his feet, he raised her by her shoulders and rolled her over, still searching for the source of blood. The back side of her was as perfect as the front. And just as bare. His gaze lingered a second longer than needed on her shapely butt before he caught himself.

He rolled her back over and pulled her gown over the triangle of light brown hair between her thighs. "Savanna?" He patted her face. "Wake up. Hey! Wake up."

Damn! Was she even breathing? He pressed his hand to her neck, her skin felt clammy but soft. Thankfully, her pulse fluttered against his fingers.

He shot up and went to the window. Her front door was open. Not a soul in sight. He recalled her one and only spoken word. *Body.*

Fuck! He ran to his bedroom for his phone and rushed back. He cut his eyes to her again, hesitating about who he should call. He went to his contacts and hit Jake's name.

"Yeah?" his partner answered, sounding groggy. Of course he was groggy, it was late.

"Got a situation. Neighbor showed up at my house, bloody, passed out. But there's no wound. Something must have happened in her house."

"Shit! Have you reported it?"

"I'd like to know what I'm reporting first."

"No, you need to . . . I'll call 'em. I'm on my way. Don't go in the house until I get there." He hung up.

Savanna started stirring. He crouched down again. "Savanna?"

Her eyes popped open. Her breath caught.

"It's okay," He touched her shoulder. "You're safe."

She gasped air in but didn't exhale.

"Breathe."

She did. She sat up. The couch sighed with her shift. "My . . . he's . . . Clint . . ."

Clint? "Something happen to your ex-husband?" A bad feeling hit. He sat down on his coffee table. Were they talking murder? Had she . . . Fuck! Her husband could be dying at this very moment.

"Do I need to call an ambulance?" he asked, sounding more like a cop than a worried neighbor.

She nodded and then the nod turned into a shake. "He's . . . dead. Oh, god!" Glancing at her hands, she suddenly lurched forward and puked. Right on his bare feet.

He stood up as it began to ooze between his toes.

She raised her face, swiping her forearm over her mouth. Her eyes widened.

"Did you two have a fight?" His own stomach turned as he moved.

She shook her head. "No. He . . ." She stopped talking. "You don't . . . ?" She dropped her head in her hands. "You don't have any clothes on." She caught her breath. "I'm gonna puke again."

Normally, his lack of clothes got a better reaction. He snagged his towel from the coffee table, where it had fallen off. He was torn between using it to clean his feet, offering it to her, or covering himself. He went with the covering himself option.

He tied it around his waist. "I was in bed." He darted into his kitchen, grabbed a dish towel, then snatched some paper towels.

When he got back to her, she had her head buried in her hands. "Here." He handed her the dishtowel. She took the towel, her hands still shaking so bad she almost couldn't grasp it.

He dropped the paper towels on the floor, scrubbed his feet against them, and then moved it to the spot that needed soaking up.

When he looked up, she had her face buried in her hands again. "Savanna," he said. "Look at me. How do you know Clint's dead?"

She moved her hands, closed her eyes, and let out a deep sob.

"Savanna? Look at me. I need you to answer me. How do you know he's dead?"

She drew in another shaky breath. "His eyes . . . were open, but he had . . ." She reached for her throat. "His throat was . . ." She threw up again, thankfully missing his feet this time.

He gave her a two-second reprieve. "Was he attacking you?" He hoped it had been self-defense.

She shook her head. "No. No."

Right then, he realized something didn't make sense. He glanced at his living room clock. It was barely five minutes after midnight. If they had fought, it had happened fast. She'd barely had time to change her clothes. And she'd come home alone. Had her ex been waiting in the house? Vaguely, he recalled the car he'd seen drive away from her house. Had someone dropped off the ex?

"What happened, Savanna?" Feeling cool air against his family jewels, he adjusted his towel again.

"I came home. I went to feed Boots and . . . he was there."

"Did he try to hurt you?"

"No." More tears slipped past her lashes. "I tripped over . . . his . . . him." She looked at her nightshirt. "There was so much blood." Her breath shook. "I turned on the light and . . ." She stopped, her mouth fell open. "Oh, my god!" She started hyperventilating again. She pressed her hand to her mouth. He moved over a couple of inches.

"What?" he asked.

"The ribbon he had . . . today I said . . ."

Ribbon? "What did you say?"

Her panicked eyes looked up. "This can't have happened." She gasped.

31

"Breathe slow," he said and asked again, "What did you say?"

She sank back into the sofa, her eyes widened with what looked like another round of panic. "I said all I wanted for Christmas was him dead with a ribbon tied around his . . . penis."

He swallowed. "Are you saying . . . Did he have a ribbon . . . ?"

Tears filled her eyes as she nodded. "Clint's dead. He's really dead. I didn't mean it. I was mad, but . . ."

Dead? Or maybe just on the brink of death. He couldn't wait any longer. He needed to make sure the man wasn't over there bleeding to death.

He ran to his room, gun still in his hand, and yanked up his jeans. He bypassed the shirt.

When he came out, she was still sitting there, a small little thing. The glow from the lamp spotlighted her. She rocked back and forth on the sofa, covered in blood, tears brightening her eyes.

"I'm going to make sure we don't need an ambulance. You stay right there, okay?"

She nodded, but he wasn't sure she heard him.

He walked out with one question filling his head. What the hell had he gotten himself into?

• • •

Mark moved into her house. The heater was on, warmth inviting him in, but he held his gun tight. He listened. Not a noise. When he got to the large family room, he stopped again. A light was on in the back bedroom that looked like the master. Then he heard something. A subtle rustle of someone or something shifting. Her ex wasn't dead. Or was someone else here? He backed against the hall wall.

His heart thumped. He counted to three then moved in. There on the bed was a gray long-haired cat. A red ribbon dangled from its mouth. Was that the ribbon that had been . . . ? Probably, he decided, when he saw the bloody paw prints splashed on the white down comforter.

The cat meowed.

Mark moved around the bed to the bathroom, thinking the body could be in there. No body. Just a nice clean scent of something fruity. He'd smelled the same scent on her tonight when she'd been in his arms.

Easing back into the bedroom, his gun out, his gaze shifted from the closet to the door. The cat looked at him, dropped the ribbon, and then swatted at it. Probably destroying evidence, but he was more worried about the blood and where it came from.

He moved back into the living room. The light in the kitchen showed just enough for him to see the bloody footprints on the light wood floors. Tiny foot prints. Savanna's footprints. The coppery scent of blood filled his nose. Shit. Could he be wrong? Had she killed her ex-husband?

One step into the breakfast area of the room and a wave of cold air brushed his bare back. He looked over his shoulder. The window was broken, glass littering the kitchen table. Had someone broken in? Her ex?

He moved to see around the line of cabinets separating the room, his gaze following the trail of bloody footsteps. Then suddenly, he saw the naked body of a man about his age lying in a pool of blood, his hands trapped behind his back. Mark started to check for a pulse, but his gaze caught on the slit throat and the victim's open eyes. Dead eyes.

Mark had seen it enough. Seen death. But he didn't think he'd ever get used to it.

Stepping closer, he looked for clues, for evidence. There, in the sink, was a large knife. Not a kitchen knife, but some kind of a hunting knife. He moved just a hair closer, careful not to step in the blood around the body, to see if he could spot any bloody fingerprints in the sink, and that's when he heard it.

This time it wasn't just a slight rustle. Footsteps. Someone was in the house. Correction, someone was in the living room.

Chapter Five

Mark swung around and saw the gun before he saw the person. His trigger finger twitched, his adrenaline spiked, then he recognized the face.

"I could have shot you!"

"I told you not to go into the house alone," Jake bellowed.

"Since when do I do what you say?" Mark lowered his gun the same time Jake did. "I thought he might still be alive."

Jake's gaze lowered to the body. The same death-is-ugly look Mark had felt reflected on his partner's face. "I'd say that's a negative."

"Did you go to my place first?"

"Yeah, she said you had gone to call an ambulance." Jake put his gun in his shoulder holster. Jake moved in a few steps to peer in the sink. "Did she do it?"

"No," Mark said. "The window's broken. She hadn't been home but a few minutes when she came screaming over to my place."

"It looks as if he was killed here." Jake studied the body. "But he doesn't look as if he's been dead that long."

Mark ignored Jake's implication that Savanna could be guilty only to hit on another thought. "I heard a car driving away an hour or so ago. I'll bet that was the killer. He probably pulled the car far enough in the drive to come in through the window."

Jake arched an eyebrow. "You wouldn't happen to have gotten the make and license, would you?"

"No." He searched his brain for the memory, remembering how he'd known it wasn't Savanna's car. "It was a medium-size car. A Malibu, I think."

Jake looked back at the window. "How would he have gotten our vic inside if he was alive?"

"Forced him through the window, maybe?" He walked over to the broken window, and sure as hell . . . "Yup. There's blood here. He probably pushed him through and then climbed in himself."

Jake looked at the blood. "Or she killed him and then broke the window to make it look like someone else did it."

Mark shook his head. "I'm telling you, she didn't do this. But . . ." He remembered what she'd said earlier. "She knows who did."

"How do you know?"

He told Jake about the whole ribbon thing. "It's in the bedroom."

Jake shook his head. "You know the Piperville cops are going to like her for this."

"Yeah," he said.

"Ahh, crap. You ran a check on this guy today, right?"

"Yeah," Mark said. " I was just checking . . ."

"It doesn't matter what you were checking. This is gonna bite you in the ass."

Mark wanted to deny it, but he couldn't. His ass was gonna get bitten. "I'll just have to prove them wrong . . . on both accounts." He started walking out, aware he'd left Savanna alone long enough.

"Wait," Jake said. "Let's talk about his."

Mark looked back. "About what?"

"I don't want you to get in any deeper. Let the

guys showing up investigate this. Don't try to be her hero until we're certain she's really innocent."

"I am certain." At least his gut said he was. Mark frowned, not liking being caught up in this.

Jake frowned. "Look, I don't know her, but neither do you. And if you look at this logically, her husband screws her out of her car, she gets all pissed, and now he ends up dead in her house. I'm just saying this doesn't look good."

Mark's gut clenched. "She didn't have time to do this. I saw her pull up and walk inside. Alone."

Jake didn't look convinced. "She could have done it earlier and left."

"I would have heard her like I heard the other car."

"What? You sat by your window waiting for her to come home?"

He hated how it sounded, but he admitted the truth. "Yeah, sort of."

Jake's frown deepened. "But . . . you didn't say you saw it pull up. You said you saw it pull away. That means you could have missed her, too."

"I didn't," Mark insisted, at least he didn't think so. He ran a hand over his face. "And, damn it, you saw her. She's maybe five foot five." He motioned to the vic again, who was at least six feet and two hundred pounds. "She couldn't have subdued that guy to get his hands tied up."

Jake's brow arched. "Maybe she's into bondage. Seriously, the guy's naked. She could have asked him to let her tie him up. As you said, I've seen her, and if I was single, hell, I'd probably have let her tie me up, too."

Mark resisted that logic even knowing it could be true. "I'm not buying it."

Jake exhaled. "I'm just saying don't jump in the middle of this, play it cool until you know for sure. If you're in the Piperville cops' faces, it'll just make you come off like a jealous boyfriend."

"I'm *not* her boyfriend." He started out and then swung around. "Oh, and don't forget, if this gets my ass in a sling, you're the reason she came knocking on my door to start with!"

He walked off, wanting to talk to her before she got pulled away from him. And they would pull her away. Separate and conquer. He knew the game. He'd played it a hundred times. Only this time he'd be on the opposite side.

"This is so screwed up," Jake said as Mark shot out the door.

And Mark couldn't help but agree.

• • •

Sweat had the back of Savanna's legs sticking to her neighbor's leather sofa. Then again, it wasn't just her legs sweating. She felt a few drops rolling down her brow. She wasn't even hot. No, she was cold. And sweaty. And half numb, half fuzzy.

Clint was dead. Clint was dead on her kitchen floor. Her breath caught again.

The words floated through her mind. *I want my ex dead with a ribbon tied around his pecker!* Clint was dead because of something she'd said. It had to be, right? But who? Who would have done this? Her hands started shaking. She looked down and saw all the blood. Her stomach roiled again.

She closed her eyes. The image of him, his blood

pooled around his body, his hands tied behind his back, and his neck slashed, flashed on the back of her lids.

He was dead.

She remembered when she first met him at Bethany's party. They had spent hours talking. She remembered how he'd come into the florist shop the next day and asked her what was her favorite flower, and that afternoon her competitor had delivered her a dozen daisies. She remembered she'd loved him.

Then she remembered how in less than a year after marrying him, he'd become angry all the time. Then with emotional clarity, she recalled coming home after her mom had passed and finding him in bed with his intern. In their bed.

`She *had* loved Clint. She didn't anymore.

But she hadn't wanted him dead. Tears rolled down her cheek. The blood, his blood, drying on her hands made them crusty. She wanted them clean. She jumped up and ran into the neighbor's kitchen. She reached for the faucet.

"Don't do that."

She swung around. Her neighbor stood there, and for the craziest second she remembered him standing naked in front of her. At least now he had on a pair of jeans.

She looked down at her hands. "I gotta get this blood off."

He walked over to her. "I know, but the police are on their way. And if you try to clean up, it'll look as if you are hiding something."

She shook her head. "I'm not."

"I know." He placed a hand on each of her forearms. His touch felt warm.

She remembered he'd said something about calling an ambulance. "He's dead, isn't he?" Her teeth started chattering, she bit down on her lip.

"Yeah."

"Someone else was here," she muttered, just remembering.

"My partner."

She leaned in, let her head rest on his chest. Warm bare skin. "I'm so cold," she muttered. "But I'm sweating."

He wrapped his arms around her. "It's shock." His face came against the top of her head. "You'll be okay." His words were soft. She wanted to start sobbing.

She stayed there for several seconds letting him hold her. Needing to be held. She found herself trying to remember his name. Then she remembered. Mark. Mark Donaldson.

"Let me get you something to slip on." He led her through the living room and into another room. She followed, feeling somehow disjointed from her body. She kept seeing Clint on the floor. She shivered.

He stopped walking They stood in a bedroom in front of a closet.

"What color would you like? Blue, burgundy, black, or green?"

Four men's robes hung in the closet. Store tags hung from the each one.

"I don't care," she said.

He pulled the blue one off the hanger. "It'll match your eyes."

He yanked a tag off the garment and held it out for her to slip her arms inside. It was silk and looked expensive. When he started to tie the sash around her waist, his hand came against her hips and she stopped him.

"I can do that."

He stepped back. She was shaking so much, she almost made a liar out of herself. Finally, she got the dang thing tied.

She looked up, their eyes met. Concern filled his light green eyes. The moment grew awkward.

Searching for something to say, to prove to herself and to him that she was okay, she glanced back at the closet. "Why do you have four brand-new robes?"

He grinned. "My mom gives them to me every birthday and Christmas. Name me a guy who really wears one of those besides Hugh Hefner."

Her heart hiccupped. "Clint did."

"Sorry." He exhaled. "The cops are going to be here any minute."

She nodded.

"They are going to ask you a lot of questions." He hesitated as if what he had to say next was hard. How hard could it be? She'd just found her ex-husband's body.

"They are going to suspect that you did this."

She had sort of come to that conclusion by some of his earlier questions, but hearing it made it seem more real. "I didn't. I just found him."

"I believe you, but they're going to need proof. So can you tell me where you were today?"

She clutched the robe closer. "I . . . was with my friends. Then I dropped them off at the airport."

"What time?"

"Their plane left at nine. So I dropped them off at about a quarter till eight."

"Then what?"

Her eyes grew moist. "I went to the cemetery."

"The cemetery? At night?"

She nodded. Was that doubt in his eyes?

"By yourself?"

She nodded again. "My mom's grave."

"Where's it at?"

"Glencoe. An hour and a half drive. Oak Hill cemetery."

"Anyone see you there?"

She shook her head.

"Did you go anywhere else? Anywhere someone could have seen you?"

"No," she said. "Well, there was a skunk in the cemetery, but I don't think he'll count."

He paused again. "Earlier you mentioned what you said about the ribbon. Who was there?"

The names started to roll off her tongue and she realized these were her friends. "They wouldn't do this."

"Can you give me their names?" He walked to a desk and snagged a piece of paper and pen.

When she didn't start listing off names, he frowned. "Savanna, you're going to tell the cops and if you tell me I can hopefully help solve this quicker."

She listed off the three names. He wrote them down.

"Wait," she said, it wasn't just them. "The waiter, Leonardo and then . . . Juan. Oh, God." Another wave of panic shot through her. "He actually said he'd hire someone to do it for me."

"Who's Juan?"

"The restaurant owner of Juan's Place."

He jotted down notes as she talked. "Why would

he say he'd hire someone to do it?"

"He's asked me out a couple of times." She paused. "But . . . I don't think he would . . . I mean, he's a nice guy."

"Did you ever go out with him?" he asked.

"No."

"Good." He looked back down at the pad. "Your friends, are these the people you took to the airport?"

She let go of a deep sigh. "Yes. See, they couldn't have done this."

"We don't exactly know what time . . . it happened."

"But I was with Bethany and Jennifer all afternoon."

"You were with those two, but not . . ." He looked at his note pad. "This Mandy Adams woman."

"No, she left to finish packing."

He tapped the pad with his pen a couple of times. When he looked up he appeared to be about to ask something, then sighed.

She swallowed another knot of panic. "You really think they are going to believe I did this?"

"Yes. Sorry."

"Mark?" a voice called out.

"In here," Mark called then he looked at her. "That's my partner."

They started walking out, her in the lead, then she suddenly remembered . . . She stopped and turned around. He ran right into her. He grabbed her by the shoulders as if to steady her, then stepped back.

His touch, even through two layers of silk, felt warm. She pressed her palm to her stomach, feeling nervous. "I got gas."

43

His eyes widened. "You . . . need a bathroom?" He pointed to the room off the hall.

She blinked and her mouth fell open. "No. Not me. For my car. You asked if I went anyplace else tonight. The receipt's in my purse."

"I thought . . ." He held out his hand, chuckled, then ran a hand over his mouth. If she wasn't still half numb, she might have thought it was funny, too.

"That's great," he said. "What time?"

"I don't know. On the way home. About a block from the cemetery."

His smiled widened — they went back to that awkward silence, staring at each other. Sirens in the distance filled the moment's stillness.

"That's good," he said. "I think we got you off the hook. Now let's see if I can convince them I didn't do it."

"Why would they think that?" she asked.

"They always suspect any guy involved with the vic's ex."

She shook her head. "But . . . we're not . . . involved."

He frowned. "We are now."

And he didn't sound happy about it.

His partner stepped in the hall.

Mark handed him the pad. "Check into these names." He looked back at her. "Where did you say your friends were going?"

She blinked. "Vegas."

"Do you remember the flight number?" he asked.

She shook her head.

"Airline?" he asked.

"United."

"Time they were supposed to fly out?"

"Eight ten, I think."

"Good." He jotted something else down, and then handed it to his partner. The man looked at the paper, his eyes widened, as if what he read surprised him, and then he looked back at Mark and nodded. "Got it."

"Got what?" she asked.

But the knock at the door ended that conversation and started a whole different one. One between her and the lead detective. One that landed her at the police station for hours. One that landed her getting pictures taken of the blood on her hands, knees, and gown. One that landed her losing her clothes and wearing prison garb.

Chapter Six

Two hours after arriving at the police station, Mark was told he could leave but to watch his step. He walked out and dropped down in a seat in the Piperville Police waiting room beside a sleepy-looking Jake. "You didn't have to wait."

Jake leaned forward and raked a hand over his face. "You'd have waited for me."

Mark shrugged and smiled. "Probably not."

Jake shot him one of his famous go-to-hell smirks. "How did it go?"

"Easy, thanks to you knowing the guy," Mark said. Jake had gone to the academy with the lead detective and they'd remained friends over the past few years.

"He didn't read you the riot act for running a check on the vic?"

"A little, but I had a legit reason. My neighbor said the guy stole her car."

"Right." Jake sounded about as convinced as his Homicide Detective buddy, Tom Hinkle. And Mark knew the shit he'd get for this wasn't over.

"You ready to get the hell out of here?" Jake asked.

"Not until they release Savanna," Mark said.

Jake frowned. "Surely you're smart enough to know you need to back away for a while."

Yeah, Mark knew that, but that quick peek he'd gotten of her, looking all kinds of vulnerable, walking back into the detective's office wearing a prison jump suit, had him deciding to throw caution to the wind. Obviously, they'd confiscated her gown for evidence. He couldn't blame the detectives, it was protocol, but she'd looked like a whipped puppy and he'd wanted to scoop her up and take care of her.

If she ended up calling someone, or having some guy show up to take care of her, he'd back off. But if she didn't, he was here. And it had nothing to do with the fact that he'd seen every sweet inch of what that bulky jumpsuit hid. Hell, for that matter she'd seen him naked, too—and said she felt like puking, but that was insignificant. She was his neighbor and she'd come to him for help—twice. The first time he'd pretty much been an asshole. This time he planned to do better.

Mark ran a hand through his hair. "Did you check and see if I was right about the name on the list I gave you?"

"Yeah." Jake said. "You were right. Did you tell Tom about it?"

"Nah, I wanted to be sure first. Besides, if she got on that plane like Savanna said, she couldn't be our killer. They're saying the time of death was around ten."

Jake rested his hands onto his knees. "Yeah, well, there's a problem with that."

"What?" Mark asked.

"I got bored so I did a check on the flight. It was canceled due to weather."

"Shit!" Mark said. "Did you inform anyone else of this?"

"No, I thought I'd drop it on you first. But we're going to have to tell Tom soon. The next flight, if they rescheduled, is in four hours. "

Mark exhaled. "Let me get her out of here first so they don't hit her with this."

Jake grimaced. "You're already up to your nose hairs in this," he said. "You need to stay clear of her for a few days at least." He shook his head and then exhaled. "But you're not going to, are you?"

"Probably not," Mark said.

"Okay, get her out of here. But I've got to let Tom know this. We can't let the suspects get on that plane."

• • •

"You are free to go, Mrs. Edwards," Detective Ross said. "But I need to advise you not to leave town for the next few weeks."

Savanna's heart gripped. She'd answered every one of his questions. She hadn't argued when asked for her nightshirt, or when the female detective handed her an orange prison jumpsuit. Orange was so not her color. Plus, Mark Donaldson and his partner Jake Baldwin had even supplied her receipt for gas across town, which proved she hadn't done this. Yet Mr. Ross still didn't believe her.

That stung. She popped up from her seat and walked out of his office into the waiting room. Walked out so fast that she didn't even stop to think that while she was free to go, she didn't have a car. Not her Honda or her rental car. And even if she did, she couldn't go home. She'd been informed she wouldn't be able to return there for a few days, maybe as long as a week.

She didn't even have her purse, so she was penniless and credit-cardless and wearing orange prison garb. Add to the fact that all her best friends were probably playing dollar slots in Vegas right now, and Savanna just wanted to fall onto the cold tile floor and weep. Not that she would. No. She'd do what she always did. Pull up her big girl panties.

But that thought only lead her to realize she was also pantiless.

Tears stung her eyes. She tried to figure out which of her employees at the flower shop would mind an early-morning phone call to come pick her up the least. Before the door swished closed behind her, she saw Mark Donaldson. Sitting across the room, he had his smart phone in his hand reading something. Beside him was his partner, sound asleep. Mark's blond hair looked mussed, and his light green eyes tired. He glanced up, looking almost guilty.

"You okay?"

She blinked back a few tears. "They think I did it." Her voice shook.

"No, they don't. If they thought you did it, you wouldn't have gotten out of there so quickly."

"I've been in there for three hours!"

"They can legally hold you for up to forty-eight. Three hours is nothing."

She remembered seeing one of the detectives taking him into another room.

"They don't think you did this, do they?"

"Let's just say I'm not their lead suspect." He smiled almost sympathetically.

"That would be me, right?"

He nodded. "The good news is that by tomorrow they'll probably be looking at someone different."

"He said he was going to go talk to Juan at the restaurant. But . . . I don't think Juan would have done that." The image of Clint filled her head again. Her breath shuttered in her lungs.

Mark moved closer. "You okay?"

"Yeah, I just . . . see . . . him in my head every few minutes."

"That's normal," he said.

She swallowed. "There's nothing normal about this."

"True." He paused. "Did they ask about your friends?"

"He got their information, but since they're in Vegas he said they weren't really suspects." She brushed her hair off her cheek. "Would you mind loaning me your phone? I need to get a ride . . . to somewhere." She paused and felt another wave of desperation hit. "And I need my purse. My keys. My rental car. Clothes." Her voice shook. *I need my mother.* The thought ran through her mind. "I need to wake up from this nightmare."

He stared at her. Probably thought she was battier than bat shit. "Look, why don't you just come home with me? Tomorrow, I imagine they'll turn over your car and you'll be able to grab some clothes and stuff."

She shook her head. "I don't want to bother you anymore."

"It's not a bother, and besides . . . there's something we need to discuss."

"What?" she asked.

He paused. "Let's go back to my house first."

She searched her mind for a reason to refuse his offer. But she didn't search too long, or too hard. She hadn't looked forward to calling one of her employees and explaining this. And since her friends were hundreds of mile away, her employees were the only people she had.

"You sure?"

"Positive." He reached out and rubbed her forearm. His touch caused emotion to tug at her heartstrings. She looked away before he saw the swell of tears in her eyes. He was being nice. She didn't recall exactly when he'd gone from jerk to nice, but she appreciated it.

Right then she remembered the other nice thing he'd done. "Crap!"

"What?" he asked.

"I need to get your robe. I left it in the—"

"Don't worry."

"But they don't need to keep it." She looked back toward the door. "I had it in the office, I just forgot. . ."

"I don't need it."

"It was a gift from your mother." She turned to go get it.

He caught her. "Savanna, seriously... I have three more at home, and in a week it's Christmas and I'll get another one. Probably a striped one this time."

"But it's expensive," she said. "I know, because I saw the label and I bought Clint . . ." His name rolled over her lips like glass. She caught her breath.

Mark's hold on her elbow, softened and his thumb started moving in little circles. "It doesn't matter. If you go back in there, they might start asking more questions. Let's just go." He met her eyes. "Okay?"

The thought of more questions won her over. "Okay."

He looked back at his partner. "Let me wake him up."

As he walked away, she saw it again. Clint's body. She wrapped her arms around her orange prison jumpsuit and hugged herself. This was so going down as one of the worst nights of her life.

• • •

She was still hugging herself when she walked into his house. Two police cars were still parked in front of her house.

"What are they still doing at my house?"

"Police work," he said.

She cringed. "Have they taken him . . . away yet?"

"I think so." He motioned toward the sofa. "Sit down. You want something to drink?"

"No, I . . . I just want . . ." She looked down at the bright orange scratchy fabric and then at her hands. They had let her wash up briefly, but she wanted a shower.

He must have read her mind. "I've got a T-shirt and some boxers. And you can shower if you'd like."

She looked up.

"Not that you don't look good in the jumpsuit. You're the . . . best looking person I've seen wearing one of those." He smiled.

She forced herself to smile back. "A shower would be good."

He took off and returned in a second with the items. "The bathroom's right through the hall. Towels and washcloths are out."

As she turned, she suddenly felt something soft at her ankles.

"Boots?" She leaned down and scooped up the animal. "How did he . . . ?"

"I brought him here right after they took you. He would have been in the way. I put his litter box in the back bedroom."

She met her neighbor's green eyes, almost the

same color as her cat's. "Thank you. I should have thought about him."

"You kind of had a lot on your plate."

Hugging Boots, she looked up and spilled her soul. "Is this my fault? I said I wanted him dead with . . . Oh, God, it is my fault."

"Hey." He moved closer and looked her right in the eyes. "People say things all the time. I wish I were dead. I'll pinch your head off. I'll kick your ass. Saying something isn't a crime. Doing it is. If someone heard you, and it seems they did, then they are one sick individual to believe you meant it, much less do it. Do not put this on yourself."

She felt a few tears slip down her cheeks. She gave Boots another soft pat, then set him down to go shower.

She scrubbed her hands and knees extra hard. In her mind, the crusty feeling of blood clung to her skin—just like the remnants of guilt. She knew Mark was right. She hadn't meant what she said, but she'd still said it.

After the shower, after seeing Clint's image a good three times, she got out and got dressed. The shirt hung to her knees. The boxers were so big, she twisted one end and knotted it. She'd give anything if she'd donned a pair of panties under her nightshirt before she'd . . . before she'd found Clint's body.

She glanced in the mirror. *You're the . . . best looking person I've seen wearing one of those.* His words floated through her head. The man was either blind or a good liar.

Giving her hair a good finger combing, she walked out, hopefully to find a place to lie down. She doubted she'd be able to sleep with the constant images flashing in her head, but he needed to sleep.

Right then, she recalled he'd told her he had something to talk to her about.

Stepping into his kitchen, she smelled coffee. He was getting out two cups.

"I thought I'd make some." His gaze moved over her, then back to the mugs. "Want a cup?"

"No, thank you. My stomach's still queasy." She paused, recalling being sick earlier. She watched him fill one of the cups and actually shook her head, finding it odd to have memories fill her head, memories that she didn't recall until right then. Oh Lord, had she really thrown up on him?

Then she remembered again what she'd hurried out to ask. "You said we needed to talk about something?"

"Yeah." He motioned to the table and then sat down himself.

She joined him then saw him look at the clock. "I'm sorry I've kept you up all night."

"No. I wasn't . . . it's not that," he said and he seemed to struggle with the words. "About your friends, the three girlfriends."

"Yes."

"Jake checked, and their plane was delayed due to bad weather. The next one doesn't go out for another couple of hours."

She sat up. "Bethany and Jennifer are still here?"

He nodded.

"Why didn't you tell me? I could have called them. I didn't have to come here. They would have come to get me."

He turned the steaming cup in his hands. "I don't think that would have been best. Since they didn't leave for Vegas, they'll be considered suspects."

She shook her head. "But that's crazy. They wouldn't do that. And besides, you said you were a suspect as well. And I'm staying here."

"Yeah, but as soon as. . ." He paused as if remembering something. "You asked about Bethany and Jennifer just now . . . you didn't mention the other one."

Boots brushed up against Savanna's leg. She dropped her hand and passed her fingers over his gray fur. "That's because she isn't . . . as close. I've known Jennifer and Bethany since junior high."

"How well do you know Amanda Adams?"

"She worked with Bethany at the law firm a couple of years ago."

"She's a lawyer?" he asked.

"Bethany is. Mandy was a receptionist at Bethany's office. They sort of became sort-of friends and she invited her to join our group because Bethany thought we needed a perspective of someone who hadn't grown up with us and wasn't so close."

"Group?"

"Not an official group. Just a . . . support group kind of thing. Two years ago when Bethany got her divorce she heard about some women forming support groups. She said it was cheaper than seeing a therapist. So she got us together and now we meet twice a month, whine, and then offer each other insights." *And I'm going to need a really long lunch to cover everything that has just happened.*

Realizing she was just staring at the table and had

stopped talking, she looked up. "Why are you asking about Mandy?"

He exhaled. "Are you aware that she was dating your ex a while back?"

His question floated around her mind. She shook her head. "No, Mandy barely knew Clint."

He glanced down at his cup and then up. "It appears she did."

She tried to wrap her head around why he would say something so crazy. "How. . . Why would you believe I . .? That's ridiculous."

He sipped his coffee. "After your car was impounded, I ran a check on your ex. Someone from his address called the cops a couple of months ago for a domestic dispute issue. The name on the report was Amanda Adams."

Savanna remembered Mandy calling Clint good looking and an asshole. Her chest felt hollow.

"I'm sorry." He set his coffee down. "I know that might be hard to hear."

"No, it can't be right." Then Savanna recalled that a couple of months ago Mandy had gone MIA on the group. Bethany thought Mandy was seeing someone, maybe a married man, and was embarrassed to admit to it. But then Mandy came back, and all she'd said was that she'd been busy, and everyone let it go. Had Mandy been dating Clint then?

Savanna's disbelief faded. Yet accepting Mandy would date Clint was one thing, but . . . "Even if she was dating him, she wouldn't kill him. She's not crazy."

He turned his cup. "Not all murderers are crazy. I know."

Savanna sat there trying to come to grips with this. "But if you're right, why would she bring him to my house to . . . do it?"

His gaze filled with empathy. "Because she hoped people would think you did it. And if you hadn't stopped for gas, and if I hadn't seen you come home alone, you'd still be at the police station being interrogated."

She swallowed. "Mandy and I aren't close, but I don't see her trying to set me up for murder." She started shaking again. "I need to call Bethany."

He set his phone down on the table. "You can use mine, but I don't think that's wise. Jake was informing one of the detectives about the canceled flight as soon as we left. Chances are, your friends have already been contacted."

"Then I've really got to get in touch with Bethany." She reached for his phone at the same time it rang. She pulled her hand back.

He looked at the screen and took the call. "Mark Donaldson," he said.

She heard a feminine voice reply.

His eyes widened and he put his hand over his phone and looked at Savanna "I don't have a clue how she got my number, but Bethany wants to talk to you, too." He handed her his cell.

"Hello." Savanna's chest clutch.

"Savanna? Oh, God, are you okay?"

"Someone killed Clint." Her eyes stung again. "In my house. I came home and found him."

"That's what the police said. I'm on my way to the police station now. Are you still there? If so, don't talk to them. Tell them you want a lawyer."

"I already talked to them." She looked up at Mark. He stood and went to the coffee pot for a refill. When he turned around she got a visual flash of him in front of her, completely naked. And just like that, she knew it had actually happened. She felt her face heat up.

"Do they think you did it?" Bethany asked.

Savanna pushed back her embarrassment. "Yes, maybe . . . Hell, I don't know. Mark says because I have a gas receipt across town I'm probably clear."

"Mark's the neighbor cop, the guy's phone I called?"

"Yeah. How did you get his number?"

"I dated a cop a few times last year. He's one of the cops on the case. He called me, and when I insisted to know more he gave me a Jake Baldwin's number. Mr. Baldwin gave me this number. Is your neighbor still being a jerk?"

"No." She glanced up and saw his eyebrow arch and realized how loud Bethany sounded. He could probably hear everything. "He's being nice."

"Where are you?" Bethany asked.

"At his house."

Bethany inhaled. "The cops want me to come in and talk to them. When I'm done, I'll pick you up. I have no idea how long it will be, though. Are you okay for a while?"

"Yeah." Savanna remembered Mandy. "Are you alone?"

"Yeah. Mandy and Jennifer were still packing their stuff. I was frantic to leave in case you needed me."

"Were all of you together last night?" Savanna looked up as Mark leaned in closer.

"No, the airlines agreed to put us up for the night in a local hotel. They gave us our own rooms. We went to the bar and had a drink and then we all went back to our rooms and crashed." She paused. "Why?"

Savanna took a deep breath. "Did you know Mandy was dating Clint?"

"What?" Bethany said. "No."

"Supposedly, there's a police report. Someone called the cops at Clint's place because of an argument between him and his girlfriend. The report claims the girlfriend was Amanda Adams."

"Oh, shit!" Bethany said.

Savanna closed her eyes and saw Clint's image again, but forced herself to ask. "Do you think she'd kill Clint and make it look like I did it?"

Chapter Seven

"You should take one of the bedrooms," Mark said after she'd hung up. "That sofa's not sleepable."

She looked ready to fall apart again. She also looked sexy as hell in his boxers and shirt, but he tried not to notice. Tried not to remember what she looked like naked. But now it wasn't just the physical that drew him to her. The quick Internet search on his phone had revealed a few things that made him want to know more.

"It's fine. Bethany should be here soon."

"It's not going to be soon. The A-team shift comes on at seven and they'll want to question her, too. You should rest."

She pressed her hand on the sofa. "This feels fine." Her cat, one of those fancy Persian cats with a pugged nose, circled her feet.

He nodded. "You sure you don't want something to drink? Milk, juice, tea."

"No, my stomach is still shaky." She looked down at the floor. "But thank you," she said, instinctively polite.

"For what?"

"For being nice."

"After I was a jerk." He recalled what he'd heard.

She flinched as if guilty. "I'm sorry, I—"

"Hey. I'm teasing."

She frowned. "You were kind of a jerk with the car thing."

"Yeah, sorry about that."

"Don't worry. I think you've more than made up

for it." She made a funny face. "I sort of recall puking on you." She offered him a weak smile.

"Right between my toes." He grinned.

Her smile widened, but still didn't reach her eyes.

"I guess we're even, huh?" he asked.

She nodded, her smile vanished. She gripped her hands. Another flashback, he suspected. He'd had them with the first three bad homicide cases he'd worked. The images would just pop into his head causing an emotional kneejerk. Sometimes, if it was bad, he still got them.

He stepped closer. "You know what you need?"

She glanced up, her face lacking color. "What?"

"A drink."

"I tried coffee at the police station. I couldn't—"

"A real drink." He walked over to a cabinet on the far side of the living room. "I have some brandy." He glanced over his shoulder. "My dad always does better at picking Christmas gifts than my mom. It'll make the flashbacks disappear."

Her eyes widened. "How did you know . . . ?"

"It's part of shock and seeing something . . . not pleasant."

He pulled out the brandy and two glasses but waited for her to say yes.

She rubbed her hand over her bare knees. Pretty knees. Pretty legs.

"You really think it'll make them go away?" she asked.

"It worked for me."

"Then I'll try it."

He poured them both a glass.

Walking over, he sat down beside her and handed

her the glass. He held up his drink. "To better days."

She took a sip and looked down at the glass. "Not bad."

She took another sip. When she pulled the glass away from her lips, they were wet. And sexy. He had his own flashback, but the good kind, of perfect skin and a curvy body. Of nipples the same color as her lips. Guilt pulled at his conscience. He shouldn't have enjoyed that. But the moment he'd found no wounds, he'd lost his protect-and-serve attitude and went straight to just being a man.

The silence felt awkward, so he asked, "How's the florist business these days?"

She titled her head. "Did I tell you that?"

"No, I . . . Googled you while I was waiting for you in the office."

"Our lives are open books now," she said. She tapped her glass with her finger. "The business is growing every year."

He noted her light pink fingernail polish. Everything about her was light. Her hair, eyes, how she'd felt in his arms when he'd carried her to his sofa.

"So what else did Google say about me?" she asked.

"Interesting stuff." He sipped his brandy. "You graduated with a degree in business five years ago—which puts you about twenty-eight or twenty-nine. You opened your shop three years ago—after managing another flower shop for two years. It led me to the article about how you donate flower arrangements to the women's shelter twice a year because your father used to work there before he died in car crash when you were a teenager. You host a Valentine's Day essay contest about what's special about your girlfriend and give away twenty-five arrangements to the winning guys. You donated your mom's home to the feral cat organization last year." He grinned. "Oh, and you also have a porn site."

Her eyes popped open. "There's a porn site with my name on it?"

"Well, they spell Savanna with only one 'n.' But don't worry, she's not nearly as pretty as you."

She choked on her drink then smiled. "You checked?"

He shrugged. "I'm a cop. Investigating is what I do."

"Right." Her smile was the first real one she'd offered him and damn if his chest didn't feel lighter seeing it.

She took another sip of brandy. "Who knew Google could tell my life story."

"That's not your entire story. I'll bet you still have a few secrets."

"I don't know, it just about covered it."

It wasn't an invitation to ask questions, but he decided to make it one. "I don't think so. For example, are you a real Texan? Born and raised?"

"Yup. Grew up in downtown Magnolia."

He nodded. She had the personality of a small-town girl. He liked that. "Siblings?"

"Only child. Which most people think means I'm selfish. And I'm not. But I'll admit, I never liked sharing my toys."

He chuckled. "How long were you married?"

From her expression, he knew this question wasn't so well received, but he'd found himself wondering about her relationship to the vic and how a guy could be stupid enough to lose her.

"Not quite two years," she said.

"What happened?"

She hesitated. "Mom was in hospice and I was staying with her. He'd been with me, but said it was too hard, so he went home." She finished off her brandy. "Mom died and when I came home, he was in bed with one of his employees."

"Ouch!" he said.

She looked at her empty glass. He took hers and replaced it with his.

"Thanks." She took another sip and her shoulders relaxed. "I stayed angry for months. And then it just . . . went away. I knew I was over it. Over him. But I didn't want . . . this to happen to him."

"I know," he said, leaning a little closer to let his shoulder brush against hers.

She exhaled. "I'll bet this whole mess will be up on Google in a few days."

"Probably," he said. "Nothing's safe from Google."

The room quieted again. She stared at the glass. "So if I Googled you, what would I discover?"

"That I don't have a porn site." He grinned.

Her smile returned. But damn, he'd thought she was pretty from across the street. Up close she was . . . Pretty didn't begin to describe it. And she didn't even have makeup on.

"And?" she asked.

He'd started this game. Now he had to play. He regretted it.

"Well, I started out a military brat. Lived all over."

"Started out?" she asked.

"My father moved into politics. So I spent my junior and senior high years either flying from country to country or in Washington."

"What countries?"

"About fifteen different ones. You really want me to name them?"

"Yeah."

So he did. All fifteen of them. Starting with Angola and ending with Venezuela.

"Wow. So cool. Your dad must have been successful." She held up the brandy. "Especially considering this and the silk housecoats you don't wear."

"He was."

"That's really neat."

He was surprised she didn't ask for titles. "Not so neat. Wealthy yes, not neat.""

"Why not?"

"Let's just say dysfunctional comes in all different income levels."

"Sorry," she said.

"Don't be. I'm fine." And he wished he hadn't said anything.

She turned her cup in her hands. "College?" she asked.

"Yes."

"Where?"

"Harvard."

"I'm impressed. Degree?"

"Criminal justice and law."

"You're a lawyer?"

"No. I'm a cop. I didn't take the bar."

"Why not? Afraid you wouldn't pass? I hear it's really hard."

"No. I'd have passed."

She tilted her head to the side and studied him. The shadows of panic were gone. The brandy had worked.

"Hmm," she said. "I don't know if that means you're cocky or just really smart?"

He laughed. "Probably a little of both, but mostly smart."

"So you were the smart, rich kid?" There was a tease in her voice.

He liked hearing it, too. He grinned. "Yeah."

"So why didn't you take the bar?"

"It wasn't what I wanted to do."

She looked at him as if surmising. "So your parents wanted you to be a lawyer?"

He reached for her glass and took his own sip, then placed it back in her hands. "Yup. Then I would follow my father into politics."

"You still should have taken the bar. I mean, if you're really smart, you should go take it now."

"Why?" he asked, disappointed that she was saying what the rest of them said. Being a lawyer held prestige. A cop, not so much.

"Because you earned it. You went to school."

"I'm perfectly happy with what I do."

"I didn't say become a lawyer. You should never do what you don't want to do. I said pass the bar. Hang the certificate up on your wall. It's something to be proud of. Bethany had to take it twice." She made a funny face and pressed a hand to her mouth. "Don't tell her I said that. She'd kill me."

"I won't," he said, enjoying the relaxed Savanna more than he thought he would.

"So you don't get along with your parents?" she asked.

He leaned back on the sofa. "We tolerate each other better."

"That's good. Having lost my parents, I think you should work on that."

"Were you close with yours?"

"I was a daddy's girl and lost him. Mom stepped up to the plate. She was more like a friend than a parent. Not that it was a bad thing. I didn't need a parent. I couldn't be bad—not after we lost dad. That nearly killed her, and I don't think I ever did a bad thing after that. Well, she didn't approve of the men I dated. She didn't like Clint at all. She was right."

He didn't know what to say, so he just listened.

"I still miss her so bad. Tonight, or last night I guess, was the first time I've been back to the gravesite." She fell against him, just a little.

He saw her eyelids droop, and he knew that between the brandy and no sleep, she was crashing. The glass settled in her lap. He took the glass and set it on the coffee table then leaned back. The lack of sleep and the little brandy he'd consumed was getting to him, too.

"You really should go stretch out on a bed," he said, seeing her eyes grow heavy.

"No." Her eyes fluttered open. "Besides, your shoulder is more comfortable." She leaned against him.

He knew then just how much the brandy had gone to her head.

"You don't mind if I . . . lean on you, do you? I haven't . . . had anyone to lean on in a long time."

"Not at all." He raised his arm to the back of the sofa so her cheek pillowed into a softer spot. A few stands of her hair caught in his five o'clock shadow.

She snuggled closer, pressed her face between his arm and shoulder. "You smell good."

He lowered his head and inhaled the fruity scent of her shampoo. "So do you."

• • •

The sound of the doorbell chased away the sweetness of sleep. But another sweetness took its place. Mark was stretched out on the sofa. Savanna on top of him. And damn if she didn't fit in the all right places. Her head cradled in the soft spot of his shoulder. Her soft breasts against his lower chest. Her pelvis pressed against . . . Oh, yeah, sweet. And a certain southern body part seemed to agree with his assessment, too. He was morning hard and then some.

The doorbell chimed again and he realized instead of enjoying this he should find a way to solve it before she woke up and found him hard and ready.

She stirred. Too late. She pushed up on his chest, looked him right in the eyes.

"Crap," She started scrambling to get up. Her thigh shifting up and down his shaft, only made his predicament worse. Or it did until her urgency to get up had her knee swinging up making a direct hit to his family jewels.

He moaned, his earlier problem now a limp non-issue.

Her gaze shot back to his face and reddened. "I'm sorry, I didn't mean . . ." She scrambled to her feet.

He tucked his hands between his legs and moaned as silently as he could.

The doorbell rang again.

"That's probably . . . Bethany."

He tried to sit up, but couldn't. Damn, she got him good.

Swallowing his moan, he heard her open the door and forced himself into a sitting position.

"Hi," he heard Savanna say. Hands still between his legs, pain all the way in his gut, he glanced toward the door. Jake Baldwin stood there, staring at him, a box of donuts in his hand.

"You okay?" Jake asked.

Was his expression that bad? Probably. He nodded.

"I'm . . . I'm . . . Excuse me." Savanna took off.

Mark watched her hotfoot it out of the room, his t-shirt swishing around her legs. Then he noticed Jake watching as well. No doubt assessing the fact that she was wearing Mark's clothes. Not that he cared all that much. His balls throbbed too much to care.

Mark lowered his head and breathed through his teeth, waiting for the pain to subside. Gripping his hands tighter between his legs, he heard Jake move closer.

"You look like you got kneed in the balls," Jake whispered.

Mark nodded again.

"She do it?" Jake asked, surprise in his voice.

"Accident." He held up one hand.

Jake laughed. "You know, I married the last girl that kneed me in the balls." He dropped into a living room chair and set the donuts on the coffee table. "I brought breakfast."

Mark took a deep breath. The throb decreased to a dull ache. He raised his head. "What's up?"

Jake looked toward the hall. "I spoke with the lead investigator, Tom, a bit ago."

"And?"

Jake motioned toward the hall. "You were right."

Mark inhaled. "I like the sound of that. But about what?"

"She didn't do it. She's completely off the hook."

Mark shifted his legs. "They have cameras at the service station where she bought gas?"

"Yup. And the cemetery had some vandalism recently so they put up cameras. She was just where she said she was."

"Good." Mark noted the amount of light streaming through the living room window, he looked at the time. It was almost eleven. He looked up at Jake. "You got anything else?"

"They are looking hard at two people for this. A Juan Ardito and Amanda Adams. Miss Adams admitted to having an affair with the vic. She also admitted to leaving the hotel last night. She says she went to meet up with another friend. A married friend. They are checking her alibi. She's worried he'll deny it because of his wife. Mr. Ardito claims he was home alone. But he lives in one of those richified gated communities with cameras that your kind live in, and says he didn't leave. Cops were collecting the tapes."

Mark cut his eyes up at his partner, frowning at the slam against him, then he recalled Savanna saying the owner of the Mexican restaurant had a thing for her. Right then, he decided he didn't like the guy.

"But Ardito indicated that one of the other gals, a Bethany—who is a lawyer and is at the station being questioned now—came right out and said she'd kill Clint."

Mark let the info roll around his brain. "Do you know what they drive?"

"You still think the car you saw driving past could have been the perp?"

"The timing's right," Mark said.

"That might be why they want you to come back down to talk to them."

Mark's phone rang. He reached for it on the coffee table, but when he saw the caller ID, he turned it off and looked back up at Jake.

"Is that them?" Jake asked. "I told Tom I'd come tell you."

"No, but I don't know why they want to see me. I gave them everything I got."

"Yeah, but you know how this works. We just keep poking the witnesses hoping they'll give us something else."

Mark frowned. "I know, but it's a lot more fun when you're the poker and not the pokee."

Savanna's cat swayed into the room and circled Jake's feet. "Ugly cat," he said, but dropped his hand to pet it. "At least Macy's cat, Elvis, has a nose."

Yeah, the cat may be ugly, but he had a beautiful owner, Mark thought. The memory of how she felt on top of him had him wondering what might have happened if Jake hadn't shown up. Would they still be all tangled up on his sofa?

• • •

After changing clothes and brushing his teeth in his master bath, Mark walked back into the living room expecting to see Savanna. She wasn't there. Jake had made coffee and was eating a donut.

"She hasn't come out?" Mark grabbed his own donut.

"Nope."

Mark finished eating and poured himself some coffee, all the while surmising why Savanna could still be in hiding. He finally hit on a reason. "Can you call your buddy and see if I can get her in the house to pick up some clothes and personal items?"

Jake reached in his jeans for his phone. "Sure."

Mark went and knocked on the bathroom door. "Savanna?"

The door swung open. She had a desperate look on her face. "Is Bethany here?"

"Not yet," he said.

She bit down on her lip. "I'm sorry for . . . for hitting you in the wrong place."

"It's okay," he said. "Jake made coffee and brought donuts. You want to come and have a cup?"

She looked down at her shirt. "I don't really feel appropriate."

"You're fine," he said, but he liked the fact that she hadn't worried about it with him last night. Of course, she'd probably still been in shock at the time, but he wanted it to mean something.

Her face reddened. "He probably thinks we were sleeping together."

Mark grinned. "We were."

"You know what I mean."

"I know." He hesitated. "I can offer you another robe."

She grimaced. "You trust me not to lose another one?"

He grinned. "Come on." He led her back to the guest bedroom where he'd stored the house coats.

"Oh, good news. All your alibis came back clear. You're no longer their top suspect."

She bit down on her lip. "I guess I should be relieved, but considering I was innocent, I figured they'd come to that conclusion."

"Yeah, well, it's still good to have it proven." He waved toward the robes hanging in the open closet. "Color preference?"

"I don't care," she said.

He snagged her the green one, yanked the tag off, and handed it to her.

"You really should cut the tags off," she said. "You might rip it."

"I'll try to remember that when I loan you the next one," he said. "Jake's calling the detective in charge to see if I can get you in to collect some personal items."

"That would be wonderful." She slipped the robe on. She looked good in that color. "I feel so . . . homeless right now. I don't have underwear, or a toothbrush."

Underwear's optional. His gaze lowered for one second. "Not true," he said, smiling. "You're wearing a pair of my boxers."

"No offense, but I prefer my own," she said, half smiling in return.

Damn she was pretty. But she was still his neighbor. He pushed that thought away. "I think I have a new toothbrush. This way."

He saw her glance at his bed as they moved

through his room and he couldn't help but wonder if her mind had gone the same place his had. Them . . . there. Them . . . there . . . minus the underwear.

Moving into his bathroom and away from his thoughts, he reached into the cabinet and grabbed a pack of toothbrushes with one left in it. "Here ya go. And here's some toothpaste." He passed her his tube.

"Thanks."

They stared at each other for a second. "They're asking me to come back to the station for some more questions. You make yourself at home. Raid the fridge. I shouldn't be too long."

"Should I lock the door when I leave?" she asked.

"Leave?" The word tasted bad on his tongue.

"Bethany should be here any minute."

"Yeah, lock the door, but. . ." Shit! He didn't want her leaving. "You know, they should be done with your house anytime." It was a bit of a lie. They'd probably have it taped up for at least another day. "You could just stay here."

"The officer last night said it could be as long as a week."

Okay, he was caught. "I don't think it'll be that long." But the idea of having her here a week sounded good. Really good. He might even take some of his vacation days and . . . celebrate Christmas with her. He hadn't realized how lonely he'd really been until now.

He held his breath. She didn't say she accepted his offer, but she didn't turn it down. Damn if he didn't want to reach out and brush a strand of hair from her cheek. Hell, they'd drank after each other, seen each other naked, and slept together—minus the awesome sex and yes, he'd already figured out it would be awesome—but right then a simple touch shouldn't feel like crossing a line. But for some reason it did.

Probably because he didn't know where this was going. Hell, he didn't know where he wanted this to go.

"Well, uh, I'll be in kitchen. You can use this bathroom or the guest." He walked off.

"Mark?"

He looked back.

Her smile came with a ton of gratefulness. "Thank you, again. For everything."

Right then he knew, not so much where he wanted this to lead, but where he didn't want it to lead. He didn't want her leaving. Now all he had to do was convince her to stay. But how?

Chapter Eight

When Savanna walked out, her neighbor's partner was gone. Mark told her they'd already gotten permission for her to grab a few things. Savanna didn't know which was worse, to go over dressed in her orange prison garb, or in her neighbor's T-shirt and boxers that were three times too big, covered with a man's silk robe. She opted for the robe getup.

"Coffee?" he asked.

The smell filled the room. "That would be nice."

He pulled out a mug from the cabinet. "Cream? Sugar?"

"Black," she said.

He handed her the Christmas mug. Savanna's gaze shifted to the cup, her breath catching as she watched Santa on the mug lose his pants. "Where did you get this?"

"Get what?"

"The cup. I had one like it, but it broke and I was sort of hoping to replace it."

He moved closer. "Is that the one with Santa losing his pants?"

"Yeah." He probably thought she was crazy. But she didn't care.

"I think Macy, Jake's wife, gave it to me."

"You wouldn't know where she got it, would you?"

"Not for sure, but I'll ask if you'd like."

"That would be great."

After a few minutes, Mark walked her across the street. At her own door a thought hit and she stopped.

"He's gone right?" She still had the images flashing in her head — she didn't need to see it for real. She started shaking.

"He's gone." He ran a hand down her forearm. The touch was welcome, it offered the resolve she needed not to run.

Two officers met them at the door, and Mark and one of the other men followed her into her bedroom. She grabbed an overnight bag and packed some essentials. When choosing underwear she did so quickly, slightly embarrassed having male eyes on her trying to match a couple of bras and panties.

Then again, making underwear selections was no more embarrassing than waking up on top of Mark Donaldson. On top of a perky Mark Donaldson with his morning rise-and-shine ready to rock and roll. Or kneeing him in the balls, or seeing the guy naked, or puking on his feet. How about his seeing her in her bathrobe, wearing a blue mask and mayonnaise hair. Her time with him was one embarrassing moment after another.

Well, not all of them. She recalled them sitting on the sofa and talking about their parents. That hadn't been embarrassing. It had been . . . nice, almost meaningful.

Was she ready for meaningful with a guy? Her heart picked up its pace. She'd considered jumping back into the dating pool, but now that the opportunity appeared right next door, she hesitated.

Then she realized how absurd it was that her ex-husband had been killed, in her place, that she was possibly being set up for murder by someone she considered a friend, and instead of worrying about that, she was fretting over her crush on her neighbor.

She needed a reality check. She glanced over at Mark, concern for her showing in his eyes. Her stomach did that flutter thing that always happened when she liked a boy. Okay, she needed a reality check really fast.

Or maybe that was what this was all about. An escape from reality. Focusing on her neighbor was a distraction from all the other shit. In a week or two, she might look at him and not feel so . . . so fluttery.

He moved in. So close his spicy male scent filled her air space. "You okay?".

"Fine." She dropped another bra in her bag. "I just need to grab my makeup." She paused. "Oh, and my purse and cell phone."

"I think they still have your phone. I'll ask and see when you can get it back. They should do it soon since your two alibis checked out."

"Are they still looking at you as a suspect? Is that why you have to go back in?"

"No, they just want to confirm some things."

"So they think Mandy did this?"

"Both she and the owner of the restaurant—the one that has a thing for you—are still persons of interest."

She clutched the bag to her. "I can't see either of them doing it. I just can't."

"I know it's hard to believe that. But someone did it. And it was someone who heard what you said at the restaurant."

"What about just some customer?"

"They would have to have known who your ex was and where you lived."

She frowned. Another heart pounding thought hit.

Had whoever done this been in her bedroom? Had they touched her things? "This is so messed up."

He dropped his hand on her shoulder. "I know, but it'll get figured out."

She looked up. "Are you nice to all murder suspects? Is that in your job description as a homicide detective?"

He grinned. "Only the ones who wear sexy underwear." He glanced down into her drawer.

She elbowed him.

He chuckled and caught her arm. "Hey, I've already been beat up by you once today."

His fingers smoothed over the silk of his housecoat. Their eyes met. It was happening again. They were having one of those nice/meaningful moments. Not because he was flirting or talking about her underwear, but because she knew he'd said it to help her over the moment's panic. It worked, too. And she appreciated it. A lot.

"Don't leave tonight," he said. "Stay."

She hesitated. "I . . .I've inconvenienced you enough."

"It's not an inconvenience."

"But . . ."

"You can sleep in the extra bedroom, I just . . . like your company."

"But . . ."

"Okay, how about you wait at my place today. When Bethany shows up, visit with her, but stay and let me take you out to dinner and if your house isn't released yet, I'll take you to her place. Deal?"

She nodded. But for the life of her, she didn't know if it was the right thing or not.

• • •

Was it a date? Or was he just being nice? Those two questions kept whispering through her mind—along with the image of Clint.

Mark left as soon as they got back to his place. Savanna watched him leave and then went and grabbed a cup of coffee—in the Santa mug. She wondered if he'd sell it her. She stared down at the donuts and her stomach growled.

The crusty sugar melted on her lips. The soft center danced on her tongue. She went to take another bite and felt the jelly center burst. And not just in her mouth. She glanced down and saw a big plop of fruit goo on the green silk housecoat.

"Crap!" Having already lost one of his robes, the thought of ruining this one hit hard. She turned to find a paper towel when the doorbell rang.

"Bethany." She took off across the living room—fruit goo and all. She yanked open the door wanting and needing her best friend. It wasn't Bethany.

An older woman stood there. Not one strand of her gray hair stood out of place. She wore an expensive suit, matching shoes, and a frown.

"Where is my son?"

"He . . . he went to the police station."

Her gaze fell to Savanna's boobs, or maybe to the large blob of donut jelly on the housecoat she'd given her son. "I was . . . the jelly donut leaked."

"He's not at the police station. I just came from his work."

"He's at Piperville Police station. Not the one he works at."

"Please tell me they aren't arresting him."

"I don't—"

"There was a murder across the street. I'm told he's a suspect."

"I—"

"I warned my son about the riff raff he'd find in this neighborhood."

"Uhh . . ."

"Who are you, anyway?"

"I—"

"What are you doing wearing my son's robe? What? Can't you talk?"

Savanna swallowed. *I'm the riff raff.* "I'm a neighbor." Savanna prepared herself for questions about the murder.

"Are you trying to sleep your way into my son's bank account?"

Savanna's mouth dropped open. That wasn't the question she'd expected. She tried to find the proper way to tell Mark's mom that it was none of her damn business, but something about standing there, wearing the Christmas gift the woman had given her son, garnished with fruit goo, and wearing her son's underwear, left her a little insecure.

"I . . . your son has . . . He's nice, but we aren't . . ."

"Oh, my!" The older woman shook her head. Tears filled her eyes. She pressed a hand over her mouth. "I'm sorry. Dr. Brighten is right, I'm acting like a bitch."

Savanna met her gaze and found her backbone. "If you're waiting for me to argue that point, you're going to be waiting a long time."

The woman looked taken aback by Savanna's honesty. But to her credit she looked more embarrassed than angry. "I'm worried about my son. Do you have any idea how hard it is to know your son is out there chasing murderers? And then to know he's being suspected of murder?" She paused. "But my therapist said I tend to say things I shouldn't when I'm upset."

"He sounds like a smart guy." Savanna wasn't ready to forgive the woman for her rudeness, but she decided it wasn't her place to call her on it, either. "Maybe you should try to call Mark."

"I've been calling him since this morning. He won't take my calls. He never wants to talk to me."

I wonder why, Savanna thought, but kept her remark to herself.

The woman stood there staring, and suddenly Savanna realized she was being rude. "Did you want to come in?"

"No. I'll go try to find my son."

Savanna recalled Mark saying, *Let's just say dysfunctional comes in all different income levels.* Maybe she shouldn't have told the woman where Mark was. Her heart went out to Mark and she thanked God for the parents she'd had.

The woman must have read Savanna's mind or maybe her expression, because she spoke up, "I'm not always this uncouth," she said. "I love my son. He may not think I do, but I do." She turned and started back to the street where a limo waited.

• • •

Mark found Jake at the Piperville police station sitting out front as if he was waiting on him. "You didn't have to come."

"I didn't have anything better to do."

Mark studied his partner. "Better than stay home with Macy? Is there trouble with your ball-buster wife?" Mark sure as hell hoped not. He personally took credit for getting them together. Their whole relationship got off to a shaky start when Macy's brother had escaped prison, and ended with Jake making a mistake that cost him the girl. Thanks to Mark's whole billboard idea, Jake had convinced Macy to forgive him.

"No trouble," Jake said. "My lovely ball-busting wife is at Nana's house helping to cook Sunday supper. I'm meeting her there at five. And, for the record, unlike someone else in the room, I haven't had my balls busted in months." His partner got his smartass grin on. "What did you do? Slip a hand where it wasn't wanted?"

"It was an accident," Mark growled. "And I might have slipped a hand where it might have been wanted if you hadn't shown up." Even as he said it, he knew he wouldn't have. Too soon after the whole murder mess, but that would change.

"Now it's my fault you aren't getting any."

Mark's phone rang. He'd just turned it on a few minutes ago. If it was his mom, he'd turn it back off. Chances were she was calling about Christmas. He'd already told her he wasn't coming. He wanted to be alone for the holidays. Or he had until he met Savanna. Hell, maybe she'd come over and they could drink some brandy and sit on his sofa and talk, or maybe by then they might be slipping hands where they were wanted. He'd put up a tree if he knew for sure she'd come over. The idea hit that maybe he should get her a gift. But what kind of gift said, *I don't know where I want us to lead, but I'd like it to lead some-where?*

His phone rang the fourth time. Not his mom. He took the call.

"Hey, Bethany, Savanna isn't here."

"This is Savanna."

"Oh, hey." He smiled. "You okay?"

"Yes and no."

"What's wrong?"

"Your mom came by."

"Oh, shit. I'm sorry. I didn't know she was in town."

"I told her where you were. I hope that wasn't bad."

What was she doing here? "Thanks for the warn-ing."

"Yeah . . . Look, since she's in town I should go—"

"No," he said. You can't cancel our date.

"I'm sure you need —"

"I need to have dinner with you." And it was true. Mark saw Jake frown. Then his mom walked into the room. "She's here. I'll call you right back."

"Give me a minute," he told Jake.

He caught his mom's arm. "Let's walk this way."

She frowned. "Not even a hello?"

"Hello." He guided her outside, stopping by the door. "What are you doing here?"

"You're in trouble?"

"I'm not in trouble."

"You're a murder suspect."

Fury bit hard. "I'm thirty-two years old, Mom. Whoever you have spying on my ass, call 'em off. Do it now, or I swear to God, I'll sever every tie I have with you and Dad."

She tilted her chin up. "You already have. You're not coming up for Christmas."

"I told you I'd come in January for your birthday."

She blinked. "Is it a crime to care about my son?"

Mark's gut knotted as he was instantly thrown back into his childhood years. "It's not me you care about. It's how this will effect Dad's career."

His mom's eyes rounded. "That's not true."

"Too bad you can't pay someone to take the fall for this one, too."

His mom looked slapped. "It would have hurt your record, too."

"It hurt Ricardo's record more."

"He didn't have to agree to do it."

Mark was sure they hadn't left him much of a choice. But this was the first time she'd admitted doing it. She was slipping. "It wouldn't have hurt my record, because it wasn't my pot. And I think deep down you damn well know whose pot it was."

"That was over fourteen years ago. Is this worth arguing over?"

"You're right. Bye, Mom!" He turned to leave.

"Mark, please. You're all I've got."

He stopped. Why did he care? Goddamn it, he shouldn't care. But he did. He'd always felt sorry for his mom. She gave everything she had to his dad — so much so that she barely had any left of herself to give to her own son. And his dad gave everything to his career and a few mistresses along the way. Some of them young enough to smoke pot, too.

He turned around. "Look, I have to talk to some people."

"Do you need a lawyer? I'll hire one."

"No." He raked a hand through his hair. "When I'm done here, I'll call you. I'll meet you for a cup of coffee, but I have a date tonight and I'm working tomorrow." Damn that sounded bad. Sounded like his parents' son. "You should have called before you came."

"I . . . I was so worried." She hesitated. "Coffee would be good. My plane leaves tonight anyway."

He nodded.

She spoke again. "I went to your house."

He turned around. "And you were rude to Savanna, weren't you?"

She lowered her eyes. "At first. But I apologized."

Damn, his mom never apologized. She was slipping. Or was it . . . "You're not dying or anything are you?"

Her mouth dropped. "No." She blinked. "But thank you for caring. I think."

Relief fluttered through him. "Apologizing isn't like you."

"I'm seeing a therapist." She shrugged. "And . . . I actually liked her, your girlfriend. She has spunk. Is it serious?"

"She's not . . . It's too soon to tell." He looked back at the station. "I have to go."

• • •

When he walked back in, Jake was talking to the lead detective on the case, Tom Hinkle. They waved him over. "Come on, let's go in the back and talk."

Mark remembered he'd told Savanna he'd call her back, but it would have to wait.

Tom wanted Mark to go over the night and seeing the car. But this time the conversation went like three cops talking and not an interrogation.

"It was either a Ford Fusion or Chevy Malibu," Mark said. "Dark color. Nine or ten at the latest."

Jake leaned in. "Amanda Adams still looking good for this?"

Tom frowned "The lover alibied her out, even gave the name of the hotel they spent a few hours at. The desk clerk remembers them. She didn't do it."

"So it's the owner of the restaurant, Juan . . . something," Mark said.

"We're still looking at him. His car didn't leave his gated community. But Bethany Sinclair, Edwards' friend, who is actually the vic's cousin, said Mr. Don Juan said he would hire someone."

Mark nodded. "Savanna told me that, too."

"My partner is having a chat with him now. Why don't we go see how it's going?"

They walked into the small room with two-way mirrors and Tom hit the switch so they could hear the dialogue.

"I'm telling you, I was joking. I wouldn't hire a man to kill another man," the voice, slightly accented, rolled out of the intercom.

Mark stared at the man on the other side of the glass. Since he knew the guy had a thing for Savanna, he'd been hoping he would be short and fat. No such luck. The tall, muscled guy reminded Mark of a younger version of Antonio Banderas.

"Prove it," the cop in the room with the guy said.

"How can I prove it?" Juan sounded frustrated, but cooperative.

"Come in for a lie detector test in the morning."

Juan paused. This was a deciding moment. "Why not do it now?"

The cop interviewing him looked shocked. "I have to set it up."

"Fine," Juan said. "Set it up."

"Shit," Tom said. "I don't think he did it."

"Maybe he just thinks he can beat the test," Jake said.

Mark exhaled and realized Tom was right. This guy wasn't coming off like a guy hiding anything. "What about the waiter? Savanna said the waiter was there."

Tom shifted. "He pulled a double shift. Worked until after eleven."

"Then it has to be one of Savanna's friends. Shit," Mark said. "And one of them is with her right now."

"Which one?" Tom asked.

"Bethany Sinclair." Mark pulled out his phone.

Tom shrugged. "Sinclair's not capable of doing this."

Mark hesitated. "You're the cop she dated?"

Tom looked surprised Mark knew this. "We're not seeing each other now. And my partner did all the talking with her. All I did was give her Jake's phone number."

"I don't care about that." Mark hesitated to call Bethany's number. "That leaves the other friend, Jennifer Peterson."

"Yeah, but she swears she didn't leave the hotel that night. We've got someone going through the hotel cameras to check."

"Any evidence at the scene?" Mark asked.

"Fingerprints are being run, but not on the knife or the sink area. It's almost as if the perp wore gloves. There were some red fibers snagged on some of the broken window glass, but that's it." He groaned. "This looked like such a slam-dunk case."

"It is," Mark said. "It has to be one of the friends."

Tom frowned. "The only one with a known motive has alibied out."

"Maybe the motive is she was doing it as a favor," Jake added. "Savanna said she wanted it and they were just giving her what she wanted."

"That would mean one of her friends is fucking insane," Tom said. "I know Bethany personally, and I've spoken with the others—including the one who had an affair with the vic. And if one of them is whacko enough to kill without a real motive, they've got me fooled. And I don't fool easy."

"Not true." Jake chuckled. "Haven't you been divorced twice?"

"True," Tom said. "But neither of them were insane. They were just bitches."

• • •

When they left, Mark decided instead of calling Savanna via Bethany's phone, he'd just drop by the house before he met his mom. He wanted to make sure Savanna was okay. Until they caught this person, all her friends were suspects.

Tom had handed over Savanna's phone for Mark to deliver, plus, he had some good news. Tom had said they would probably be finished with her house tomorrow. He kind of hoped she'd decide to just stay at his place. Not that he planned on hitting on her. She could sleep in one of his three extra bedrooms. The image of her naked flashed in his mind and he recalled with clarity how good she'd felt on top of him.

They were adults. If they ended up spending the evening together, so be it. He wouldn't push her into something she wasn't ready for, but he wouldn't turn the opportunity down if it came.

He forced his mind back to dinner. Having only consumed donuts, his stomach grumbled. What type of food did she like? The thought of getting to know her intrigued the hell out of him.

He pulled up at his house. There wasn't a car out front. Had Bethany come and gone? Eager to see Savanna, he walked inside. The silence seemed too loud. Too lonely. When he shut the door, the sound of it echoed in the too quiet house. He should've been used to it. He lived alone and even when entertaining women, he seldom brought them home. But lately the lack of noise in his house bothered him. As if to punctuate his thought, the ice maker spit out ice and clonked in the silence.

"Savanna?" he called, hoping he was wrong.

No answer came back.

He looked around for her cat. No cat. . . He glanced in the kitchen and the donuts and coffee mugs they had left out had been put away. Had she left? Disappointment, loneliness washed over him.

To confirm, he went to see if the litter box had been taken. When he walked into the room, he stopped dead in his tracks.

Chapter Nine

Mark's breath caught with relief. On her side, she laid with her blond hair scattered across the pillow she was sharing with her gray cat. Savanna didn't stir, but the cat raised his head and stared at him as if to say, *hey, buddy, we're napping.*

Mark ignored the cat and continued to study her. She wore some of the clothes she'd brought over with her. Jeans, worn enough that the material had long learned the shape of her body. A soft looking pink sweater hugged her, not tight enough to be purposely provocative, but just the right size that it didn't hide her curves.

His gaze traveled to her legs. Barefoot, her toenails were painted the same light pink as her fingernails. She obviously didn't go for flashy or bold. She went for soft and subtle, and it looked so damn good on her.

Happiness chased off the earlier disappointment. She hadn't run off. The question hit. How had she gotten under his skin so quickly? Hell, it wasn't quick. He'd been fascinated, and fantasized about her since he first laid eyes on her over four months ago mowing her yard. Then he met her and realized she was wittier, prettier and more genuine than he'd ever envisioned. How could a man not fall hard for a woman who surpassed his own fantasy?

The cat meowed. Mark debated waking Savanna up. *No, let her rest.* He'd run and have coffee with his mom. He walked out and found paper and a pen.

Hey . . .

I found you asleep, and since I needed to run to see my

mom for a few minutes, I decided to let you rest. I got your phone for you. Call me when you wake up.

Mark

He started to put down the pen, but he decided what the hell.

P.S. You're pretty when you sleep. Think about what you want for dinner. My treat.

He eased back into the room and set the note on the bedside table beside her phone. Glancing down, the temptation to brush a strand of hair off her cheek hit strong. He poked his hands into his jean pockets and walked out. He couldn't rush this. Whatever it was.

But what did he want it to be?

Was he ready for something real again?

Hell, he'd better start figuring that out. And quick. Because that's where it felt like it was going.

• • •

Mark was about to end the visit with his mom. He'd set his phone on the table so he wouldn't miss Savanna's call.

"So you're definitely coming down for my birthday?" his mom asked.

"Yeah." He glanced at his phone, wishing it would ring.

"Are you bringing your girlfriend?"

Mark frowned. "She's not . . . It's new. "

"But you like her, right?"

"Yeah." *A hell of a lot.*

"It's not that new. She was wearing your robe." Her eyebrows rose.

His jaw clenched. "That was because . . . We haven't even had a real date yet."

She nodded. "But you're going out tonight, right?"

He frowned. "Yes, but . . . Can we change the subject?"

"Why?" she asked, sounding hurt.

"Do I really have to answer that one?" He cut her a hard look.

She fidgeted with the skinny vanilla latte she'd barely sipped. "I just . . . You haven't dated in a while. It's not normal for a man your age not to have . . . sex. You're not gay, are you?"

His head spun.. "No!"

"My therapist says that your father's and my relationship could be the reason that you don't see women."

"You discuss . . . *me* with your therapist?"

"No. I mean, not . . . Only when it pertains to how I feel about something."

"Well, stop feeling something about my sex life, would you?"

"I just want you to be happy, Mark."

He took a calming breath. "Believe it or not, right now, I'm happy." And it had a lot to do with the blonde sleeping in his extra bedroom who wasn't calling him. Much to his delight, his phone finally rang. He snatched it up. He didn't recognize the number. It had to be her.

"Excuse me," he said and pushed back from the table.

• • •

While hand-washing the silk robe, Savanna debated whether or not to call. If he was with his mom, then . . . Yet, his note had been . . . well, sweet. And she wanted to know if he'd gotten anything else on the case. So she dialed his number, feeling almost guilty.

"Hello," Mark answered. "Savanna?"

"Yes," she managed, feeling tongue tied.

"How was your nap?" he asked.

"Long," she said. "You should have woken me up."

"After the last twenty-four hours, you needed the rest."

She inhaled. "Thank you. And thank you for getting my phone."

"No problem."

"Did you learn anything else about the case?" she asked.

"They're still looking at everyone."

"You mean my friends?" she asked "They're wasting their time. They didn't do this."

"Someone did, Savanna."

"It wasn't them." She sighed.

There was a long pause. "Have you decided on what you'd like for dinner?"

She pushed her frustration aside. "How do you feel about Mexican?"

"Love it," he said. "Anything but Juan's place," he said.

"What's wrong with—?"

"I'd prefer not to take a woman out on a date to a restaurant owned by a man who is interested in her."

"He's not . . . I mean, he asked me out, but—"

"Which means he's interested in you."

"Okay," she said. "But I wasn't even thinking about that place."

"Good," he said. "How do you feel about Latin food? It's sort of Mexican."

"Sounds great." She suddenly realized what he said. "Is this really a *date* date?"

He hesitated. "Define *date* date."

She searched for a definition.

He spoke up, "What did you think it was?"

"I . . . I mean, I thought it was, but . . . it occurred to me that you could just be acting neighborly."

"I think we've passed that stage."

A thrill whispered through her. That nap must have done miracles. "What stage are we in?" Her tone came out flirty.

"Uh . . ." He hesitated. She heard the background noise lessen. "What stage is after you've seen each other naked?" he asked in a low teasing voice.

She chuckled. "I saw you naked, but you haven't seen me."

"Maybe I should tell you about that later."

"Tell me about what?" Had she forgotten something else? She searched her memory.

"I was worried you'd been hurt, so I . . . checked." He sounded worried now.

"I don't remember. . ."

"You were passed out."

She remembered wearing the white nightshirt with no underwear. "You saw me naked?"

"Maybe I should have kept that to myself."

"Probably." Though, she wasn't mad. Just embarrassed. Again.

"If it makes a difference, at the time I was just . . . concerned you were hurt."

"I guess that makes a difference."

She heard him exhale as if relieved. "I'm heading home in a few minutes. Are you up for an early dinner? I never ate lunch."

"Starved."

"Good," he said. "I'll grab a quick shower and we can go. Oh, and good news. The detective said your house should be cleared tomorrow, so you could just stay at my place."

"I think it would be best if—"

"In the extra bedroom, of course."

"Thanks. I appreciate it. But Bethany's expecting me." Savanna remembered how good it felt waking up on him. If she stayed, she might end up waking up there again, minus the clothes. And while the thought wasn't unpleasant, it seemed too soon. She really needed to test the waters before she dove into the deep end.

• • •

Mark said goodbye to his mom, paid for the coffees, and within thirty minutes was walking into his place. He hadn't stopped smiling on the way, either.

Believe it or not, right now, I'm happy.

He recalled his words to his mom. Anticipation buzzed inside him. He shut the door and looked around, eager to lay eyes on her, but even more eager to touch her. "Savanna?"

He heard the shower in the extra bath running. No

silence. He liked that. Then he stumbled across something else he liked. The mental image of her naked, standing under the warm steamy shower. Anticipation stirred below his waist.

He needed to chill. Her insistence to stay with her friend told him she wasn't ready to take it there. Most women had a three-date limit. He had a feeling she'd be worth the wait. Not that he'd complain if she waived her rules. They *had* slept together. That should count for two dates, but he didn't plan on pushing. Or pushing that far. He hadn't even kissed her, but that was going to be remedied tonight.

• • •

Savanna sipped her margarita. The sweet tart flavor combined with the salty rim exploded on her tongue. She looked around the restaurant and the clientele. Upscale. Probably five star. Not that she hadn't been in some nice places, she had. She made table decorations for a lot of the high-end restaurants, and her and her mom had made a habit of going out to some of the finer establishments every three months.

The hostess, seating another table, turned and smiled at Mark. It had been apparent when they'd arrived that the two new each other. Savanna almost asked him about it, but was afraid it would sound too nosy. Or jealous. The hostess was five stars too.

"I think I might be underdressed," Savanna said.

"There's no dress code. You look great. I'm wearing jeans, too."

"Mark, my boy. They told me you were here." A

Hispanic man in a charcoal suit and tie, his voice slightly accented, walked up to the table.

"Yeah, I thought I'd stop in for a bite to eat, Ricardo." Mark motioned to her. "I'd like for you to meet Savanna Edwards." Mark looked back at the man. "Ricardo Gomez owns and runs Mi Casa. He used to cook for my family years ago."

"What he never tells is that he is part owner here, as well. He helped me get my dream going."

Savanna glanced over at Mark. "You're right, he didn't tell me."

"I know a good investment when I see one," Mark said. "The food is to die for."

"You also know how to get the pretty ladies. Someday you have to teach me this." Ricardo smiled at Savanna.

"Thank you," Savanna said.

"What would you two like to eat? I'll fix it myself."

Mark ordered and thirty minutes later, she concluded he was right. The food was to die for. They had shrimp and chicken paella, sautéed vegetables and fried plantains, and were sharing some bread pudding with caramel and raspberry sauce.

"This is heaven," Savanna said.

"Almost. Heaven is Chili Mango Jelly Belly jelly beans," he said.

She laughed. "You're a jelly bean guy?"

"Not just any jelly bean. It has to be Jelly Belly, and the only one I'd kill for is the Chili Mango."

"What makes Jelly Bellies better than other jelly beans?"

"Obviously, you've never had them." He pointed his spoon at her.

She laughed. The conversation and company was right up there with the food and possibly as good as jelly beans. They talked a bit about his travels, his job as a homicide detective, and part ownership of the restaurant. She also found out he worked out three times a week, which explained the great abs. Abs that were now covered by a light-blue dress shirt he wore with casual jeans. The color looked good on him.

"So you bring all your dates here?" she asked, remembering Ricardo's remark about Mark dating only pretty women.

He had just scooped a spoonful of dessert into his mouth. "No."

She cut her eyebrow up at him. "Your business partner seems to know they are all pretty."

He grinned. "Actually, he's referring to my younger days. I was seventeen when he worked for my family."

She tried to envision Mark as a teen. "I'll bet you were hell on wheels."

"My biggest sin was speeding tickets."

She leaned back in her chair. "So what exactly does your dad do in Washington?"

He hesitated. "He's the White House Chief of Staff."

Savanna's mouth dropped open. "Holy crap. David Donaldson is your dad?"

He nodded. "You know a lot about politics?"

"No. But I catch the news a couple times a week so I know who he is. So, have you been to the White House? Have you met the president?"

He nodded and sipped his margarita.

She got the feeling he didn't like talking about his

family. She found that sad, but having met his mom, she figured she'd give him a break.

He pushed the plate of dessert her way. "It's your turn."

"No, I'm full."

"No, I mean, we've talked about me the entire time. Tell me about you."

She reached for her water. "You know everything. You Googled me." She smiled. "You even checked out my porn site, remember?"

He laughed and she liked the sound of it. Liked how it crinkled his eyes in the corner. There wasn't anything to dislike about this guy. Well, except him having been a jerk in the beginning.

"There has to be more," he said. "What do you do in your spare time?"

"I work and meet my friends for long lunches. I do workout at the YMCA a couple times a week at lunch." She glanced down at the dessert plate with the raspberry sauce. All of a sudden, the image of Clint and his blood flashed in her head. She closed her eyes. "And I . . . find ex-husbands dead in my house."

"Another flash?" he asked.

She opened her eyes. "How long will it last?"

"Everyone is different. But it gets less and less." He reached over and dropped his hand over hers. "You ready to go?"

"Yeah." She reached for her purse. "Can I help pay for this?"

"No, one of the perks of being part owner is free food. I just have to leave a tip." He pulled out three twenties, then grabbed his brown leather coat. Where was he when she was waiting tables to get through college?

"Thank you," she said. "It was a great dinner and company."

"I would have to agree with you," he said, his green eyes filled with honesty.

They walked out into the chilly night toward the car parked around the back. She slipped on her sweater. He dropped his jacket over her shoulders and then slid his hand around her waist. Warm tingles spread from his touch. His coat felt good; he felt good. His hip brushed against hers as they walked. Those tingles, his spicy male scent, had her wanting to get under more of his clothes. She really couldn't stay at his place.

• • •

Mark pulled up into his driveway. He should have kissed her before she got into his car. The way she'd sort of leaned against him as they walked told him his kiss wouldn't have been refused. But the parking lot hadn't been empty and he hadn't wanted an audience.

"Crap," Savanna said as he pulled into his driveway.

"What?"

"I just realized I don't have the cat carrier. I mean, unless you got it when you got Boots?"

"Sorry, I just brought him over." He hit the garage door opener. "He can stay here. It's just one night. For that matter, you can still stay here."

She shook her head. "No, I need to go, but . . . Are you sure you wouldn't mind cat-sitting?"

"Nah, I think he likes me." He released his seatbelt.

When he turned to her, he caught her staring, but that was okay. He'd done his own staring when she wasn't looking. Or when she was passed out.

She blinked. "He has good taste."

"You didn't think so at first. Or that's what you told Bethany. I think the word 'jerk' was used."

She chuckled. "You were a jerk at first."

He stared at her smile, enjoyed bantering with her, and wanted to kiss her so bad that he almost climbed over his seat to get to her.

They got out and he walked her to the porch and unlocked the door. She looked at him.

Kiss her. Kiss her now.

"I should get my things." She walked inside.

"Now?" Disappointment filled him as he watched her move down the hall. "It's not even eight o'clock." His gaze lowered to her ass. Damn but she had a body that was as good going as it was coming.

She glanced over her shoulder. "I told Bethany I'd be there around eight-thirty. They're waiting for me."

When she walked back into the living room, he met her with the bottle of brandy. "Take this in case you need it."

She frowned. "No. It's expensive."

"I have another."

"Doesn't matter," she insisted.

"Yes, it does. Take it. If you need something to help you with the flashbacks, you've got it."

She frowned. "But . . ."

He put a finger against her lips. "Just say thank you."

She took the bottle and slipped it into her bag. "Thank you."

Just as he was about to lean in, she turned for the door.

"Here, let me help you." He took her bag and walked out with her. As they crossed the street to her driveway where her car waited, he slipped his hand in hers. Her palm was soft against his. She wasn't getting away before he tasted her lips.

She hit the unlock button. Still holding her hand, he opened her door and tossed the bag into the passenger seat.

She offered him a weak smile. "Thanks again." She started to pull away, but he gave her a slight tug.

"Not so fast." He caught her around the waist and pulled her closer.

He leaned down and pressed his lips to hers.

She tasted a little like tequila, a little sweet like the dessert they'd shared. He folded his arms around her and brought her closer. Her breasts melted against his chest. He couldn't remember a woman ever fitting against him and feeling so right.

Chapter Ten

He tasted like margarita. His tongue slipped into her mouth, taking the kiss from simple to sexy. And it was so sexy. The way his hand moved up and down her ribcage.

The way her breasts pressed against his chest.

The way her pelvis fit against his.

Their tongues danced and explored each other's mouths. He pulled his lips back, almost ending the kiss, then came back a little harder. The push and pull became what made the kiss so hot. The simple motion brought on fantasies of making love—two bodies burning to find release. And she was . . . burning.

She slipped her hand behind his neck and into his hair. The next thing she knew, she was pressed against the back passenger door. His thigh came between hers. Every inch of him was against every inch of her. So close not even the December breeze slipped between them. And she still needed more.

She felt the hardness through his jeans pressing against her and realized they had to stop. Stop before they couldn't.

Slipping her hand from around his neck, she eased her fingers between their faces, their lips.

He pulled back a few inches.

"I think . . ." Oh, she could hardly think.

"Think you should go," he finished for her.

She nodded.

He pressed his forehead against hers. "Funny, that wasn't what I was thinking."

She grinned. This close, his eyes were so green and so filled with heat.

She felt it too. Her knees barely held her up.

She inhaled. "For the record, there's a big part of me that doesn't want to go."

"Then don't," he said. "Stay." He ran his hand up her waist again—never touching her breast, but making her wish he would.

She blinked. "I . . . it's too soon."

He took a deep breath and a step back. "I understand." His gaze met hers. "I don't agree, but I understand."

She nodded. Shifting to the right, she slipped into her car. Once she was settled, he leaned in and kissed her on the corner of her mouth. Soft. His lips moist.

"Think of me tonight," he whispered, his warm breath on her cheek.

She looked up. "It'll be hard to think of anything else."

His smile came off sweet, and a little sexually frustrated. "I guess it would be wrong to try to talk you out of leaving again, huh?"

• • •

Savanna pulled up at Bethany's house, her body still humming from the kiss. When she knocked, Bethany called for her to come in. Her two best friends were crashed on the sofa, wine glasses in hand—probably already a couple of glasses ahead of her.

Jennifer ran to hug her. "I'm sorry about Clint. I'm sorry about Mandy dating him." The hug got tighter. "I'm sorry you found the body. I'm sorry you were suspected of murder." Jennifer's hold loosened and Savanna gasped for air. "I'm just full of sorry."

So maybe Jennifer was about three glasses ahead.

Savanna pulled back a bit. "It's okay."

"You can't be okay after all that's happened," Jennifer insisted.

"I'm not completely okay, but . . . I'm dealing with it." And just like that, a barrage of emotions filled her chest and the image of Clint flashed. Maybe she wasn't dealing with it. "I mean, I feel almost guilty for what happened."

"Guilty?" Jennifer asked. "You didn't do this."

"No, but the cops keep saying it had to be someone who heard what I said. If I hadn't said it, then—"

"Bullshit!" Jennifer said. "Do you know how many things I've said I didn't mean? How about . . . *Just kill me now*. Well, shit, do you think I really wanted to die? Hell, I'll bet even the Pope says stuff he doesn't mean. If some fucked-up individual takes something you said literally, that just means they are fucked up."

Jennifer seldom dropped the F-bomb. Savanna looked at Bethany. "How many glasses has she had?"

Bethany grinned. "This is our second bottle, but she's right. Seriously, you can't blame yourself for this."

"I'm a wise drunk!" Jennifer said and giggled.

Savanna sighed. "Thanks, guys. I love you."

"By the way," Jennifer said. "We decided it's up to you if Mandy stays in the group. I voted to kick her ass out. But politically-correct Bethany here said the call is yours."

Savanna frowned and dropped into Bethany's big comfy chair. She hadn't dealt with the whole 'a friend dated my ex thing.' It just didn't seem all that important compared to other things.

But Savanna suddenly realized it wasn't just that. She simply didn't care. Didn't care that Mandy had dated Clint. Didn't really care that she'd lied. It did, however, say something about their friendship, though. Mandy was simply part of their group . . . never her *friend*. "I don't know if it matters."

"It matters! I mean, if she had dated Cary, I would have pinched her head off." Jennifer looked at Savanna. "See, there's another thing you can't take literally."

"She lied to us," Bethany said.

"I know, but, I'm telling you, her dating Clint is the least of my problems." She looked at Bethany, and knowing Clint was her cousin, she asked, "How is Clint's dad handling this? Is your family blaming me?" She saw an image of Clint again on her kitchen floor. She dropped her head in her hands and pushed hard against her eyelids.

"His dad is upset, but he doesn't blame you. He even said that if you were going to kill his son, you'd have done it when you caught him cheating in your own bed."

Savanna sank deeper into the chair. "Who could have done this? Who would have killed Clint?"

"He had a lot of enemies," Bethany said. "His dad said Clint and his partner in that nursery business had a falling out. And he had to fire the woman you found him in bed with when she discovered he was just using her for sex."

"But how would either of them have known what I said?"

"Maybe one of them was at Juan's place that day," Jennifer said.

Bethany stood up. "Let me get you a glass of wine."

Savanna leaned over and pulled out the bottle of brandy. "Actually, I might just drink this."

Bethany walked over and looked at the bottle. "Shit, this is good stuff. Where did you—"

"My neighbor."

"I think I'm beginning to like that guy," Bethany said.

"Me, too," Savanna said. "And that is one of my other issues."

"How can that be an issue?" Jennifer said.

"Let me get a brandy glass while you pick her brain," Bethany said.

"So why is liking this guy an issue?" Jennifer asked again.

"I don't know, it just feels . . ." She paused trying to put it into words. "My ex-husband is murdered in my house, and instead of . . . thinking about that, I'm lusting after my next door neighbor."

"Hey . . ." Jennifer filled her glass up again with red wine. "I just read an article that said grief is practically an aphrodisiac. It's a natural instinct. When someone dies we fear our own mortality, and fearing our mortality makes us want to copulate to keep the race alive. Seriously, did you ever watch the "Wedding Crashers" movie? Some guys crash funerals to get lucky."

"That's ridiculous," Savanna said.

"But probably true." Bethany took the bottle from Savanna's hands and poured some in a sniffer glass.

"So the date must have gone well?" Bethany paused. "Wait, what am I saying, it must not have gone so well, considering you're here. I was half expecting you to cancel."

Earlier today, Savanna had told Bethany about waking up on top of her hot neighbor. About how he made her feel nervous and giddy at the same time. "Are you kidding? I barely know him," Savanna said.

"And if you'd stayed, you'd be getting to know him a lot better," Jennifer added. "Has he kissed you yet?"

"Yes," Savanna said. "And I melted right into my panties."

"Ohhh, I love those kind of kisses," Jennifer said. "If guys only knew that with the right kind of kiss, a woman doesn't even need foreplay."

"I always need foreplay," Bethany said. "But a really hot kiss is a great start. You know who could really kiss? Tom Hinkle, the detective." She shook her head. "Listen to us. I think it's time we all consider dating again."

Savanna took a big swallow of brandy. It burned going down, but the warmth that followed was welcome. "My life's a mess."

Jennifer dropped back against the sofa. "At least the last guy you dated didn't show up at your door wearing a dress and a wig."

Savanna shook her head. "No, the last guy I dated and married showed up dead on my kitchen floor."

"Okay, you got me beat on that one," Jennifer said.

Bethany looked at Jennifer. "I told you when you said his legs were shaved that something was fishy."

"I want turtle doves," Jennifer said. "I want a guy

who will just love me and not cheat on me. And for God's sake, I don't want them to ask to wear my panties."

"I want a guy who isn't intimidated by the fact that I'm a badass lawyer. I want control in the courtroom, but not always in the bedroom."

Both pairs of eyes shifted to Savanna. "What?" she asked, still enjoying the brandy-induced warmth.

"What do you want?"

"I want. . ." She downed the rest of her brandy. "I want my neighbor."

• • •

Mark lay in bed staring at the ceiling and wondering how the hell she could have walked away after that kiss. It had been one of those kisses you didn't walk away from. Then again, perhaps the kiss hadn't been that good for her.

His brain recalled how every inch of her came against every inch of him. He remembered how she'd tightened her thighs when his leg went between them. Nope, she'd enjoyed that kiss just as much as he did. Running a palm over his face, he accepted she wasn't exactly in a great place emotionally right now. She might have walked away because of that.

He glanced over at his phone on the nightstand. He'd brought it in here, hoping she'd call. But why the hell was he waiting for her to call? Why didn't he call her? His gaze cut back to the clock. Midnight. Too late.

But maybe not too late to send a text. She'd find it in the morning. Or maybe she was still awake and she'd call him. He reached for his phone.

• • •

The next morning, Mark dropped down at his office desk and checked his phone again. No message. No missed calls. Disappointment pulled at his gut.

"Hey." Jake walked in.

"Hey." Mark hit a few keys on his keyboard to bring up his email.

"Where's breakfast?" Jake asked.

Shit! Mark had forgotten. They'd been taking turns bringing breakfast for almost a year. "I . . . I wasn't hungry."

"Right." Jake leaned his ass against the edge of his desk.

"It's not going to kill you to skip a meal," Mark said.

"Right," Jake repeated in his sarcastic tone.

"Shit! I'll go get you a donut!" He stood.

Jake held out his hand. "So you didn't get any last night, huh?"

Mark dropped back into his chair and grabbed his coffee, which was already half cold, and took a sip. He wished like hell he was a better liar, that he could tell Jake his mood wasn't in any way tied to sexual frustration, but he couldn't. He'd stayed up half the night thinking about what he wanted to do to Savanna in bed. In the shower. On the sofa.

Mark set his coffee down on the desk a little hard. "Do yourself a favor, and drop it!"

"Is she still at your place?"

"No. She went to stay with her friend."

"Which one?"

111

"Why?" Mark asked, hearing something in Jake's tone.

"Tom called this morning. The detective running the hotel tapes spotted the Jennifer chick leaving the hotel and she swore she hadn't. They've tried to reach her and she's not picking up her phone. She wasn't at her apartment either."

Mark took in what Jake said. "Savanna was going to see Bethany, the lawyer, but . . . Crap!" He grabbed his phone.

"What?" Jake asked.

He called her number. "She said something about "they" were waiting on her. Hell, if this woman is sick enough to kill once, she could do it again."

The phone rang three times then went to voice-mail.

He hung up and found Bethany's number. She answered on the second ring.

"Where's Savanna?" he demanded.

"She went to work. Why?"

"She's not answering her phone," he said. "Where's Jennifer? Was she with you and Savanna last night?"

"Yes. Why?"

"Where is she now?"

"Why?" The woman's tone changed, sounding like a lawyer.

"The Piperville cops are trying to find her."

"She already talked to them."

"They need to talk to her again. And they can't find her," he said not wanting to say more.

"The reason they can't find her is that she's still in

my extra bedroom sleeping." She paused. "She's not a killer, Detective Donaldson."

• • •

Savanna heard her phone ring and walked back to the front of the florist shop from doing inventory. Or pretending to do inventory. Anything to escape the worried look in Janice's eyes. Janice, one of her best employees, had freaked when she'd told her about what happened. Then, while she'd gone to make a de-livery, she'd picked up a paper. Sure as heck, there on the front page was an article about the murder and a picture of her porch with police tape hanging from the eaves.

Savanna hadn't read it. She knew it all too well.

When she picked up her cell, she noticed she had a text message she hadn't seen. She pulled it up.

Miss you.

Hope the brandy worked and you are having sweet dreams.

Mark.

P.S. Can't stop thinking about that kiss.

Savanna's heart took a tumble in her chest. She looked to see when the text was sent. Midnight last night. In spite of all the issues crowding her heart and mind right now, she smiled. She liked knowing he'd been thinking about her. Because even with her life going to hell in a handbasket, she'd sure as heck been thinking about him, too.

She checked to see who had called and she saw his number. She looked to see if he'd left a voice message. He hadn't.

Should she call him back? Text him?

For one second, she wondered if her attraction to him wasn't just pure escapism from all the crappy stuff happening. No, she realized, it couldn't be. She'd been attracted to him from the first time she'd seen Mr. Blond and Beautiful grabbing his mail almost four months ago. He'd had his shirt hanging open and was wearing a pair of well-worn jeans and she stood by the window practically drooling.

She had her finger hovering over the call back link when her phone rang. This time it was Jennifer.

"How's your headache?" Savanna asked.

"They think I killed Clint," Jennifer said without preamble.

"What?"

"I forgot I walked to the drugstore right next to the hotel to get something for my headache and they got me on tape and now they think I snuck out and killed him."

"They don't think that," Savanna said. "They can't."

"They told me not to leave town."

"Have you talked to Bethany?" Savanna asked.

"She went with me. This is so friggin' crazy."

"I'm sorry. I'm sorry you're getting pulled into this."

"It's not your fault," Jennifer said and her voice shook. "You know I hated Clint for what he did to you, but I wouldn't kill him."

"I know that," Savanna said with complete honesty. But then she heard the detective's voice in her head, *Someone killed your ex-husband, Mrs. Edwards, and it was someone who heard what you said at that restaurant.*

But not Jennifer, she thought. It couldn't be Jennifer.

• • •

A few minutes after she hung up, the bell over her door chimed. Two customers walked in. One wanted to talk about table arrangements for a Christmas party, and another wanted to talk about her wedding.

Savanna had Janice go over some possible arrangements while she spoke to the soon-to-be bride. An hour later, she had a signed contract to do another wedding, a Christmas party job, and three bouquets of flowers that needed to be made and delivered. It was almost lunchtime when she sent Janice out to deliver the arrangements and she finally got a breather. Not that she hadn't appreciated being busy, it had helped her forget. And she'd only had one flashback of Clint dead on her kitchen floor the whole time.

She went and grabbed her phone under the front counter, found the text from Mark, and started answering, when the door chimed again. She glanced up.

Her heart did another tumble when Mr. Blond and Beautiful himself walked in. When his green eyes lit on her, he smiled, but it seemed slightly hesitant.

"Everything okay?" she asked.

Chapter Eleven

"Fine," Mark leaned against the counter. He'd talked himself out of coming then back into it a dozen times. If she had doubts about whether getting involved with him was a good idea, then maybe it wasn't. He'd had a few doubts of his own, hadn't he?

Somehow he'd managed not to get to this emotional place with the women he'd seen in the past year. But was he lowering his guard because time had healed some old wounds, or because this woman was special?

But seeing her now, he was thinking it was the latter. And it wasn't just because she had every sweet curve and dip a man wanted to touch and feel against him. It was . . . the whole package. Her wit, her unpretentious approach to life, and even the fact that she owned her own business. He liked beautiful, smart, funny, down-to-earth go-getters.

And he really liked seeing her in her element. His gaze shifted around the place to the glass coolers that held a dozen different vases of colorful floral Christmas arrangements.

"You need to buy some flowers?" she asked with a smile.

"Yeah, I was wondering what kind of flowers you send a girl who you had a great date with, but when you text and call her, she doesn't answer."

"Hmm. As a florist, I'd sell you something really expensive, but because I'm thinking I might be that woman . . ." She held up her phone. "I'd tell you if you'd given her five more minutes, you'd have heard from her."

"You sure?" he asked.

"Look for yourself." She handed him her phone that held the message she'd already started writing: *Mark, I just found your text this morning and I was swamped, but I have thought of . . .*

He looked up into her soft blue eyes. "So what have you thought of?"

"You," she said.

He glanced around to make sure they were alone. "Not the kiss particularly?"

She grinned and those blue eyes twinkled with a touch of embarrassment. "That too." She sighed. "I've actually had a busy day. It kept me from . . . thinking too much."

"Well, that's a shame." He leaned over the counter and kissed her. A quick kiss. "I guess I've been thinking enough for both of us."

When he pulled back, she blinked her eyes open. "You're good at that."

"Kissing?" he asked in a teasing voice.

"Well, you're good at that, too, but I meant making me forget my life's a mess right now."

He brushed a strand of hair from her cheek. "I hope you don't consider me part of that mess."

"I don't," she said. "It's just . . . everything's happening so fast and in the middle of chaos."

In spite of thinking pretty much the same thing, disappointment curled up in his gut. "So you want to slow it down?"

She bit down on her lip as if debating. "No. I probably should, but I don't. Unless you think it would be best?"

"No, I don't." It wasn't a lie. Sure, he'd considered it, but he wasn't ready to turn his back on this. If the "being his neighbor" thing came back to bite him in the butt, he could lease out his house and move. It wasn't as if he couldn't afford it.

"Have you heard anything else about the case?"

He really wasn't supposed to tell her everything, but he told her what he could. "I think they are interviewing a couple of your friends again."

"Jennifer called me. She forgot to tell them she walked next door to the pharmacy that night. It's ridiculous. Jennifer didn't do it. She won't even spray her yard with pesticide because it will kill the lizards."

He hoped Savanna was right about her friends, because it would hurt if she learned otherwise. But as a cop, he couldn't help but think it was one of them. "They're just doing their jobs."

"They're wasting their time," she insisted.

"Unfortunately, homicide detectives have to waste a lot of time to find answers. But, I do have some good news. The Piperville police are finished with your house."

"I can go home." She blinked several times and then glanced away, and he figured he knew why. Home wasn't the safe haven it had been a few days ago.

"How about I come over and we'll figure out dinner?" he asked. "Or you come over to my place. We can do pizza or Chinese takeout."

"Sounds good," she said, but he could tell her

mind was someplace else, and he had a good guess where.

"You still having flashbacks?" he asked.

"It's happening less. But yeah."

"If it doesn't go away, you might need to see someone about it." A bell rang, announcing someone had walked in.

She bit down on her lip. "I thought you said it's normal?"

"It is, but it's hard to deal with sometimes."

"I'm a big girl," she said.

No, she wasn't, he thought. She wasn't petite, but she barely came to his shoulders, and right now she had that vulnerable look about her. The look that made a man want to rush in and take care of her. Was that what he was doing? Just wanting to take care of her?

"I hope my cat wasn't any trouble," she said in an obvious diversion.

"No, he slept with me. He's a pillow thief, but other than that we got along."

She smiled again. She glanced at her potential customer and then she refocused on Mark. He remembered something he needed to tell her. "I hope you don't mind, but . . . I went ahead and arranged for someone to clean up your place and fix the window. They came in right before the officers left. And they were just going to lock the door when they finished."

Her face grew pale. "I didn't even think about cleaning. . . I guess I just thought they would . . . I should have known that they wouldn't. Thank you. Just let me know how much it is."

"That's not an issue."

"It's not as long as I get the bill." Her gaze shifted to a woman staring into the coolers containing the Christmas bouquets.

He shifted away from the counter. "I'll see you tonight. What time do you get home?" He'd be there to make sure she didn't have to go in alone.

"Around seven," she said.

He rested his palm on top of her hand and brushed his thumb across her wrist. "See you then."

• • •

Mark walked back into his office two hours later. He'd also gone to talk to a retired cop who'd worked the Logan cold case he and Jake were just assigned to look at. Thankfully, murder wasn't an everyday occurrence in their precinct, and the further from Houston you got, the fewer bodies dropped. But anytime there wasn't a new murder, their boss threw cold cases on them. Not that Mark minded. He'd rather have a case than sit around waiting for someone to get killed. And he kind of liked solving cases that others before him had failed at. So far, he and Jake had solved three cold cases this year.

While Mark had visited with the retired detective, Henry Owens, Jake was supposed to be chasing down the old witnesses on the telephone. Mark carried in a bag from the fancy vegetarian sandwich shop down the street from the precinct. It wasn't until he almost turned into the precinct's parking lot that he realized he hadn't eaten anything all day.

"How'd it go?" Jake asked, popping his head into Mark's office.

"I took notes, but most everything he told me was in the files."

"Not the case, the other thing."

"What other thing?" He opened the bag of food he'd bought on the way back to the precinct and pulled out one of the grilled mushroom and provolone sandwiches. "Did you eat? I got an extra to make up for not bringing your breakfast. It's even vegetarian, so your wife would approve." Unlike Jake, Macy was a vegetarian.

Jake smirked. "I ate."

"Bet it wasn't vegetarian."

"I had them make the double burger a single, I figure that counts for something."

"I'll bet it still had bacon on it," Mark teased.

"Just one slice." Jake frowned. "But stop talking about my eating habits just to change the subject. I know you went to see your hot neighbor. It's written all over your face."

"Bullshit." Mark focused on pulling the paper off the sandwich. But he realized he was smiling. He looked back up at Jake and thought *what the hell*. "Fine. I went to see her. We're having dinner tonight."

"You and your neighbor?" A feminine voiced piped up from the door.

Macy moved in, dressed in a gray business suit that showed off her curves.

"Look at you. All lawyerly and everything. And showing some leg, too. Nice," Mark said.

"Yeah, the pizza uniform was better, wasn't it?" She grinned.

"You look good in whatever you wear," Mark said.

"Quit hitting on my wife," Jake said, brushing a

kiss to her cheek. "How did the interview go?"

Macy wrapped an arm around Jake's waist. "Great. I may have the job." She looked back at Mark. "That smells good. Is that from the vegetarian sandwich shop?"

"Yup. I got one for Jake here, but he turned his nose up." Mark reached into the bag and held it out.

"I'm starved! I was too nervous to eat before the interview." She grabbed the sandwich and looked back at her husband. "They said they would call me in two weeks. And their office is only eight miles from our house."

"Any firm would be crazy not to hire you." Mark took a bite of his lunch.

Macy unwrapped her sandwich. "When am I going to get to meet this mysterious neighbor? Jake said she has some spunk, so I'm thinking I might like her."

Mark wasn't surprised Macy knew this. He'd accepted a while back that anything he told Jake would get to Macy. He even kind of respected it. They had the kind of marriage he'd thought marriage should be. Not like what his parents had.

"We're just getting to know each other." He grinned. "Besides, I'm trying to convince her I'm normal. Why ruin it so soon by introducing her to you guys?"

"I don't know," Macy said and grinned. "I heard she already met your mom. So I don't think we could hurt your reputation any more." Unfortunately, Macy and Jake had the pleasure of meeting his mom when she'd stopped by unannounced when they were over watching a football game. His mom had thought Macy was his date, and the fact that she'd still been in her pizza uniform had brought out the worst in her mom.

Right then he remembered his mom telling him she'd apologized to Savanna. Had his mom turned over a new leaf? Was that possible?

"Touché," Mark said. Leave it to Macy to call it like she saw it. He realized again that in some ways, Savanna was a little like Macy. Frank, witty, and pretty. Jake was a lucky bastard. For one second, Mark wondered if he could get so lucky. "But let's not talk about my mother." He popped a fry into his mouth.

"Fine." Macy pulled the paper from the sandwich. "But, I should warn you, if this neighbor thing doesn't work out, Nana's been asking about you."

Mark nearly choked on his french fry. "Hey, your grandma's cute, but I don't think we're compatible," he said and chuckled, remembering the old lady trying to get him to join her yoga class at Jake and Macy's last barbeque.

Macy laughed. "Sorry, you're not her type either. She wants to fix you up with her boyfriend's grand-daughter. She said you had a lonely aura that she felt compelled to heal."

"So now she's doing yoga and healing auras. Does she read palms, too?" Mark asked.

"I think she took a class on that once." Macy grinned.

"Don't laugh," Jake said. "Ninety percent of what that woman says is right on the mark. Plus, she cooks me pot roast on Sundays."

Macy rolled her eyes. "If the devil served you pot roast, you'd love him, too."

"Only if it had the little potatoes and carrots in it." Grinning, Jake came over and snagged a few fries from Mark's bag. Then he grabbed the sandwich from Macy and took a bite. "This ain't bad. It's not pot roast, but it's better than a tofu burger."

"So you really like this girl?" Macy asked Mark.

So much it scares me. "I don't know, it's new."

"He's lying like a big dog," Jake told Macy. "When he came in a few minutes ago, he had a shit-eating grin, AKA I'm-gonna-get-lucky grin, on his face. He hasn't grinned like that since I've known him." He took another bite of the sandwich.

Mark was about to argue the point when he remembered something. "Hey, you know that cup you gave me last week, the one where Santa loses his pants when it gets hot?"

"Yeah," she said and popped another fry into her mouth.

"Where did you get it?"

Right then, Mark's desk phone rang, as well as his cell. Jake's phone went off, too.

"I guess that means lunch is over." Macy frowned. "And I'll bet you'll be late for dinner, too."

When Mark looked at the number on his phone, he knew Macy was right. They were being called to a scene. He looked at the clock. It was almost two. New cases usually took four to six hours. Hell, he hoped this was a slam-dunk. He had to be back at his place by seven, come hell or high water.

Jake answered the call. "Yes. What's the address?" He grabbed a pen from Mark's desk and snatched the notepad. "We'll be right there."

Mark stood up. Jake kissed Macy. "See ya later."

As they walked out, Jake looked back at Mark. "Oh, I forgot to tell you, Tom called me before you got here. Guess who didn't pass the lie detector test to-day?"

"Seriously? Don Juan didn't pass?"

"Well, Tom said he didn't completely flunk it, but it was inconclusive. They're getting a court order to look at his bank records to see if he pulled out any substantial amounts of cash that could have been used to hire a hit."

Mark sighed. "I'd rather it be him than one of her friends. Then again . . . Shit. Did they tell Savanna?"

Jake pushed open the door, leaving the precinct.. "I don't know."

"Someone needs to tell her. If he's crazy enough to hire someone to kill her ex, he's crazy enough to hurt her."

Mark pulled out his phone and called her. It went to voicemail. "Hey . . . it's Mark. The cops are still looking at Juan Ardito as a suspect. So . . . avoid him. Got it?"

• • •

It was after five and both hell and high water had come. This was no slam-dunk case. They had a mur-der scene without a victim. Correction, they had a scene, not officially ruled a murder scene, but with the amount of blood, chances were somebody was dead, or in the hospital getting transfusions.

After studying the blood, Mark actually called to see if the local hospitals had treated any bad wounds. No such luck.

And since the home's resident, Nick Curley, was missing, they assumed the bleeder could be him.

A young girlfriend of the late twenty-year-old man, had come by to check on him when he hadn't showed up for work that day. They both worked at a local grocery — her as a cashier and him as an assistant manager. When she found the blood on the living room floor, she'd called the cops. Both Jake and Mark had spoken with her and neither liked her for the possible crime.

They also found a gun in Mr. Curley's bedroom, but it didn't appear to have been used recently. They looked for evidence of a shooting and found none.

"What do you think? Knife?" Jake asked.

"Possibly. Fatal wound, too. It looks to be about as much blood as there was on Savanna's kitchen floor." Mark continued to stare. "And the blood pattern sort of looks similar."

Jake looked up. "You aren't thinking they're connected, are you?"

"No," Mark said surmising the odds. "That's not likely." He returned to the kitchen and asked the girl-friend a few more questions. "Nick have any enemies?"

"No. Well, his ex and him were always fighting. They had a huge argument over the phone a couple of days ago." Tears appeared in her eyes. Mark got the ex's name. He and Jake would be paying her a visit before they called it a day. Which would mean he'd miss being there when Savanna got home. Damn.

"Was Nick into anything illegal? Gambling or drugs?" Mark asked her.

"No," she insisted.

Mark pointed out that he'd found a small bag of marijuana in the bedroom.

"Fine, he smoked a little weed, but that's all."

All the neighbors who'd been home during the day swore they hadn't seen or heard anything out of the ordinary. Mark and Jake waited until most of the crime scene photos had been taken, then they left to find the ex.

No one was home at Mrs. Curley's house. The ex's place, a small, older house in Piperville, looked like a rental.

"Hmm," Jake said. "The hubby's living a better lifestyle than the wife. It could cause some hard feelings."

Mark and Jake separated and knocked on doors asking neighbors about Mrs. Curley. They got the usual—she was a nice, quiet woman with twin boys. Not that this lessened the suspicion. More times than not, the nice, quiet people ended up being murderers. And more times than not, it ended up being the ex.

Then again, not always. It wasn't in Savanna's case.

Mark met Jake back in the front yard. "You get anything?"

Jake closed his notepad. "Lady across the street said that Mrs. Curley is out of town for a few days visiting her mom. I asked if she ever mentioned her ex and the neighbor said Mrs. Curley was upset when she left and mentioned she'd had an argument with him."

"But was she mad enough to kill him?" Mark said. "And what would she've done with the body?"

"Don't know, but she left yesterday, the blood at her ex's house was dry, so the timeframe could still fit.

However, the neighbor is dog-sitting for the ex-wife. She says Curley called and checked in on the dog. Sounds as if she's actually coming back. I got her cell phone number. We need to have a chat with Mrs. Curley."

Yeah, they needed to do that. Mark checked the time, it was now six forty-five. He'd expected Savanna to call him about Juan, but then again, she was working. He needed to call her to let her know he'd be late. The thought of her having to walk into her place alone had his gut clenching.

• • •

Savanna turned off the lights in the shop. She let her gaze wander. The sense of pride she felt at owning her business, and being successful at it, was still there, but she had to dig for it under the other emotional baggage taking residence in her heart.

Today her emotions were so up and down and back and forth. The thought of Clint being dead had her feeling guilty for no longer loving him. The thought of seeing Mark had her feeling . . . anticipation, and yet the thought of trusting someone like she'd trusted Clint scared her. Then when she heard Christmas music it had her thinking she needed to go shopping for her friends, but it also reminded her of what she wouldn't be buying this year. A crazy Christmas mug for her mom.

She'd just gotten into her car when her phone rang. She checked the number. Mark. And just like that, the anticipation hit. She remembered the hot kiss and the magical feeling that had chased away the doom and gloom when he came into her shop.

"Hello?"

"Hi." His voice rang deep and sexy. "Where are you?"

"Heading home. Am I late?"

"No. I've gotten caught up in a case and it'll be an hour before I get home. You want to just hang out at work for a while longer?"

"Why?" she asked, confused.

"I . . ." He paused. "I assumed it would be easier to go into the house if I was with you. I'd hoped to be there."

He was right. Walking into her house alone was going to be hard. The fact that he cared, was sweet, but . . . "Thanks, but I've got to face it sooner or later."

"Later is sometimes not a bad idea."

"I'll be okay." It was probably a lie, but as much as she anticipated getting to know him, she didn't need to start emotionally depending on him. Slow and easy. And yet there was nothing slow about the kiss he'd given her last night. And nothing easy about the decision she had to make tonight. Whether to let him kiss her like that again. Because if he did, it wouldn't stop at a kiss.

Could she do that and not be emotionally dependent? She knew Bethany, Jennifer, even Mandy, had come to the place that they didn't view sex as serious. Unfortunately, Savanna hadn't arrived there yet. Or she didn't think she had. Tonight might be the test.

"Did you get the message I left earlier?" he asked.

"You didn't leave one," she said.

"I did. I called you around two this afternoon."

"I'm sorry, I must have missed it. It's been a busy day."

"No problem, but I just wanted you to know that they are still looking at Juan Ardito. So stay clear of him."

"I don't think . . ."

"I know you don't think he did this. But just humor me."

She hesitated. "I will."

"I'll call you as soon as I get home. I'll take a shower and I'll be over. You aren't starving, are you?"

"No."

"Good," he said. "I can't wait to see you."

He hung up. She realized she needed to shower, too. She reached down and ran two fingers under the hem of her jeans. She also needed to shave her legs. And she'd do that, just as soon as she got home and stopped freaking out about her ex-husband being killed in her kitchen. Holy hell, she thought. Was she ready to be tested?

• • •

Savanna's hands shook when she pushed open the door. The air smelled like astringent, like a hospital. It reminded her of her last week with her mom. It reminded her she was alone. Even Boots wasn't here.

She closed her eyes and fought the image from forming. Too late. She saw it in her head. Clint dead.

Clint lying in a puddle of his own blood.

To prove the image only existed in her mind, she forced herself to move into the kitchen. Heart pounding, she could swear he was there, that's how strong the mental image flashed. Blinking until it faded, she stared at the white tile.

Inhaling a shaky breath, she took off for her bedroom. The bedspread with Boot's bloody tracks was gone. She dropped on her bed, missing her cat, missing her mom, missing feeling safe in her own home. She took several minutes to just sit there before heading to her bathroom. One question echoed in her mind. Who had done this? Who had killed Clint?

The hot water and steam felt good. So good, that twenty minutes later, she hadn't left. When the water lost its heat, she decided to get out. She almost forgot to shave her legs, but stepped back under the lukewarm spray.

Job, done, she got out, combed her hair, and found her best underwear, which weren't all that sexy. She hadn't done sexy in over a year. She donned a pair of soft-fitting jeans and a light blue, long sleeved T-shirt. After drying her hair, she put on mascara and lip gloss.

She padded through the living room. The chill of the wood floor came against her bare feet, but shoes were a habit she kicked off when inside.

She hesitated before turning into the kitchen. Her heart pumped in her throat. The house felt too quiet.

"He's not there," she muttered and forced herself to move. Forced herself not to listen to creaks of the heart coming on.

• • •

Mark watched Jake put the phone on speaker and dial Mrs. Curley's cell number. She answered on the third ring. "Hello?"

"Mrs. Curley?" Jake glanced at Mark.

"Who's this? My caller ID says the Attalla police."

"I'm Detective Jake Baldwin," Jake answered. Mark eased himself into the chair across from Jake's desk.

"I'm broke, can't donate to your charity."

"I'm not calling for donations. It's about your ex-husband."

"Was he drinking and driving again? He can rot in jail."

Mark glanced at Jake. Mrs. Curley was either a damn good actress or she didn't know about her husband's disappearance.

"No, ma'am," Jake said.

"Is something wrong?" she asked.

"Your ex-husband didn't show up for work, and when a friend of his went to his apartment, she found a large amount of blood."

"Blood? Is he okay?"

"He's missing. So we can't be sure of that."

"What are you saying? I mean, what do you think is going on?"

"We're not saying anything. We hoped you might be able to tell us where he is."

"No . . . I'm at my mom's in Dallas. I haven't spoken to him since Friday."

"Do you know where he could be?"

"No. Wait, he's dating some college kid who works at his grocery store, but . . . I don't know her name or anything." She sighed. "Should I come home?

If you think something has happened, maybe I . . . Oh, God, you don't think he's dead, do you?"

• • •

"This is crazy," Savanna muttered to the dark house. She saw the empty floor and couldn't look away. Sighing, she went to the counter and hung on. She was going to beat this. She had to.

Her stomach grumbled. Probably from nerves, but since she'd hardly eaten today, she decided hot chocolate might hold her over.

She reached in the cabinet where her Christmas mugs were stored. She saw the Santa cup—the one like Mark's. Even though the handle had broken, she hadn't been able to throw it away. It had been the cup her mom gave her on her last Christmas. She passed her finger over it, vaguely recalling the laughter they'd shared. Then she reached behind it for the one that played "Jingle Bells" every time she picked it up.

Adding a double portion of marshmallows, she went to sit on the sofa. She'd only drank a couple of sips when her doorbell rang. Mark had obviously forgotten to call.

She didn't care, the idea of not being alone really appealed to her. Moving to the door, she peeked out just to be sure. All she saw were flowers. He'd bought her flowers. Her anticipation blossomed as she opened the door. But as soon as she did, and the flowers lowered, Savanna saw her mistake.

It wasn't Mark Donaldson at her door.

Chapter Twelve

When Mark pulled into his driveway, he spotted the Porsche parked in front of Savanna's house. Did Bethany drive a Porsche? Then he noticed someone stood on her porch. Not just someone. Juan Ardito.

Unsnapping his gun holster, he bolted across the street. By the time he got to her front lawn, he had his hand on his gun. He heard Savanna's voice and realized her front door was open. Hadn't he told her to stay away from this guy?

Savanna stood at the door in front of Don Juan, who held a big bouquet of flowers.

"Hello," Mark announced himself.

Juan turned. Mark kept his hand on his gun. The flower-toting man didn't make any sudden moves.

Savanna's gaze shifted to him. Relief flashed in her eyes. "Mark," she said.

"Can I help you?" Mark slipped between the huge bouquet and Savanna. With the tension easing from his shoulders, Mark dropped his hand from his gun.

"I brought Savanna flowers," the man said, calmly.

"Yeah, well, since you're still a suspect in her ex-husband's murder, it isn't wise for her to accept them or for you to be here."

"I'm not a suspect."

"Yeah, and I'm not a cop, either." He pulled out his badge and flashed it.

The man went speechless.

"So, adios." Mark shifted back, bumping into Savanna.

"I'm sorry," Savanna said over his shoulder. "Thanks. We'll talk when this mess is cleared . . ." Mark shut the door. "Up."

Frowning, he turned around. "Didn't I tell you to stay away from him?"

"I thought he was you."

"That's why you have a peephole," he said, annoyed she'd told Juan they'd talk. Was she interested in Don Juan or just being polite?

"I used the peephole. All I saw were flowers. And I thought you'd brought me flowers."

Shit! Should he have brought her flowers? "I didn't bring . . . I was working a case. Sorry."

She shook her head. "I didn't mean . . . I wasn't expecting you to bring 'em, but you'd mentioned buying flowers today at the shop."

He nodded. "Well, you shouldn't open a door without knowing who's on the other side."

"I figured that out as soon as I realized it was him." She didn't sound angry at his unsolicited advice, but she wasn't remorseful either.

"Did he say anything to frighten you?"

"No. I was just nervous because you told me the police still suspected him."

"You should be nervous," he said. Then he realized he wanted to start over. This wasn't how he'd planned the evening. He'd wanted to grab a quick shower and then show up and pull her in for another hot kiss.

"Are you hungry?" he asked, trying to change the subject and the mood of the evening.

"Getting there."

He noted she'd changed clothes. Even this far away, he could smell her shampoo. "Have you decided what you'd like to eat?"

"The Chinese place around the corner is good."

"You want to call it in while I shower?"

"Sure. I have their number on speed dial. What do you like?"

"Cashew chicken. Egg rolls. Fried rice. And whatever you like." He moved a little closer. "I'll see you in a few minutes."

She smiled. "Can you bring Boots when you come?"

"I don't know, after sleeping with me, I think he might want to stay." He smiled. He recalled she might be nervous about being alone in her house. "Would you like to come over to my place?"

"I'm fine. I have to learn to deal with it," she said.

He admired her for not completely lying. She was having a hard time, but was determined to overcome it.

"Okay, but lock the door and don't answer to anyone. Unless it's me."

"What about our Chinese food delivery?" she asked.

"I should be here before they deliver." He gazed at her mouth.

Moving in, he lowered his head and his lips met hers. He'd meant the kiss to be simple, like the one they shared at the florist, but something happened. He wasn't sure if he'd done it, or if she had. But soon, their tongues were dancing and they were both holding on to each other. She felt good. So good, the need for a shower seemed like a distant memory.

The ring of her phone was a little like a cold shower. They pulled apart. She reached for her phone on the coffee table, turned it off, and then looked up at him. "Bethany. I'll call her back."

He nodded. The taste from her kiss lingered in his mouth. He ran his tongue over his bottom lip. "Chocolate?"

She stared at him a second, confused then smiled. "Hot chocolate." She picked up a cup from the coffee table. "Jingle Bells," started playing from the dish.

"Musical cup?" His body hummed from the kiss.

"Christmas cup," she said.

So she had a thing for Christmas cups, did she?

They stared at each other, the tension sweet, but slightly awkward. "I'm going to go shower, I'll be right back. "You sure you don't want to come with me?"

Her eyes widened. "To the shower?"

He grinned. "Well, you could, but I meant just to my house."

She cut her eyes toward the kitchen. "Seriously, I've got to get over it. I live here."

"Okay. . But order the food. I'm getting hungry." Yet he wasn't as hungry as he was eager to get his hand under that cotton T-shirt, or to slip those jeans off her curved hips. It was going to be a quick shower.

• • •

When someone knocked, she looked through the peephole. It was Mark. The few minutes he'd been gone, she'd spent trying to decide if there was a downside to letting this happen. And yes, she'd found a few, but the upsides won over. Mainly, she was tired of being alone.

She opened the door. He held her cat in one hand and a bottle of wine in the other. Thankfully, Boots was the kind of cat that went limp when you picked him up.

Mark studied her. "Did you look through the peephole?"

"Yes." She reached out and took the cat from his arm and gave him a good scratch under his chin. Boots immediately started purring.

"Good." He leaned down and kissed her quickly.

He tasted minty fresh. Boots wiggled in her arms.

"I need to go back and get his litter box."

"Oh, there's another one in the extra bedroom. We can get it later." She set Boots down.

He nodded. "I brought a semisweet Riesling. I think it would probably go with Chinese, but my wine matches are sometimes off."

"Sounds perfect." She took it from him. "Food should be here soon. You want to start with wine?"

"Sure."

She started into the kitchen. And stopped when the image flashed. He came up behind her and wrapped his arms around her.

"It's okay," he said softly.

"I know." She let go of a deep breath.

"We could go to my place."

She leaned her head back against his warm chest and looked up at him. "He took my first house from me. He took my car. He even robbed me from being able to grieve in the right way for my mom. I'm not letting him take this house." She closed her eyes. Guilt whispered over her heart. "I'm sorry. It's not nice to talk badly of the dead."

"I didn't hear anything bad," he said. "Just honest."

"I really didn't want him to be . . . hurt. I just wanted him out of my life."

"And for good reasons," he said.

She walked further into the kitchen and grabbed two wine glasses from a cabinet. "I'm breaking one of the big rules."

"What rule?" She noticed how good he looked. His blond hair appeared a little darker, as if still wet. He wore faded jeans and a dark green t-shirt that clung to his chest and shoulders. She had a quick mental visual of him without it. Her heart raced a bit faster when she realized she'd probably be seeing that again tonight.

"Don't talk about your ex on a date."

He shrugged. "I think our situation is different considering . . . everything."

"I guess." She grabbed a wine opener from the drawer.

"Here. Let me do that."

She watched him open the wine and suddenly the question hit. "Have you ever been married?"

He looked up. "No."

"How did you escape that?"

"By the skin of my teeth," he said.

"You were engaged?"

He nodded.

"What happened?" she asked.

He arched a brow. "What was that rule about not talking about exes?"

She frowned. "It's just . . . you know all about me."

He unscrewed the cork from the wine opener. "Let's just say she didn't like my chosen career."

"She didn't want you to be a cop?" All of a sudden she remembered. "She wanted you to be a lawyer."

"Yup."

She bit down on her lip. "Was she afraid you'd get hurt working as a cop?"

"I think she was afraid having a cop for a husband was below her standards."

"So she was rich, huh?"

"Not really, but she wanted to be, hence her reasons for wanting me to become a lawyer."

"Sorry." Then the question just slipped out, "Did you love her?"

He reached for the glasses and filled them. "How about we nix the talk of exes and talk about ourselves." He handed her a glass.

"Okay." But she couldn't nix the feeling that he might still be in love with someone else. Was that not another downside? "Why did you want to be a cop?" she asked, when the silence grew.

He sipped the wine. "Well, I didn't like politics, didn't want to wear a suit and tie and argue cases in a courtroom, and yet I still wanted to help people solve their problems."

"Do you solve people's problems?"

"Yeah. Well, sometimes I do." He frowned. "Don't get me wrong, I also get an inside view of some seedy sides of life. But there's generally someone involved who doesn't deserve the bad crap happening to him or her. And when that's the case, it sort of feels good."

"So, what do you do when you're not playing cop or restaurant entrepreneur?"

"I don't do much at the restaurant. I just helped Ricardo get the startup money."

"Were you two close when he worked for your parents?"

"Yeah. We lived in Venezuela. He was our cook and part-time chauffeur. He used to take me and my friends around for joy rides. He taught me how to drive."

Savanna got the feeling Ricardo was more of a parent than the ones Mark was born to. "So, what else do you do for fun? Sports? Read?"

"I'm like all guys. If it has a ball involved I'm interested. Football, soccer... Jake and I meet up for some basketball a couple times a week."

"So, you and Jake are really good friends, too?"

"Yeah, but he's a pain sometimes. He married Macy about three months ago. He met her right after we hooked up as partners. She's good for him." He took another sip of wine. "She said she'd like to meet you. If you wouldn't mind."

"That'd be fun." She turned her glass in her hands. "And books? Do you read?"

"I love a good book. I've read all the Harry Potters and James Pattersons. And the first four chapters of that *Shades* book." He made a funny face. "I still don't get why you women would like that."

She laughed. "If it makes you feel any better, I never finished the first one either."

"Good." He smiled. He gazed into her eyes. "Oh,

and lately I've had this crazy fascination with my neighbor."

"Really?" She found it easy to get lost in his light green eyes.

"Really." He inched closer. So close, she could smell the shower-fresh scent on his skin. He leaned down. His lips brushed against hers. After a few seconds, he put his glass down and took hers and set it down, too. He held her so close that there wasn't an inch of her that didn't press against an inch of him. His hands came around her waist and his fingers slowly moved under her sweater to touch her bare skin. She couldn't remember a simple touch feeling so seductive. All she could think about was his hand on other body parts. Her breasts felt tight, swollen.

She let her own hands wander, slipping her fingers under his T-shirt to touch his back. He moaned. His knee came between her thighs, pressing against some very sensitive areas.

Then the doorbell rang.

They pulled back, both a little breathless. "I'll bet that's our dinner," she said.

"Yeah." The doorbell rang again. He passed a finger over her lips as if to collect the moisture his kiss had left. "We should probably open the door."

"Probably." She grinned.

She followed him into the living room. He walked to the door and then glanced back. "See? This is how you look through the peephole." He pressed an eye to the tiny hole. "It's a Chinese guy with carry out, or I wouldn't open the door."

She grinned. "But in all the movies, he's usually the guy with the gun."

"You can't believe anything that happens in the movies."

He opened the door and pulled out his wallet. When he was told the dinner was already paid for, he looked back at her and frowned. She just shrugged.

He gave the guy a bill from his wallet. She wasn't sure, but it looked like a twenty. No doubt the guy was going to be doing cartwheels when he left.

He took the bags and shut the door. "Why did you pay? I'm the one who suggested it."

"You paid for last night's dinner."

"It was free," he said.

"Right, I saw the tip you left." She waved to the living room. "Set it on the coffee table and I'll get us some plates." She left to get the dishes.

"No," he said when she handed him forks. "When you eat Chinese, you eat with chopsticks." He pulled out the two plastic covered chopstick sets.

"I'm terrible at using chopsticks."

"You just haven't had anyone teach you."

He showed her how. And she still sucked at it. He fed her and she tried to feed him. They laughed when most everything she tried to feed him ended up on his T-shirt. "I'm ruining your shirt," she said.

"We could both take our shirts off," he said with a sexy twinkle in his eye.

She elbowed him.

"I guess that's a no."

She finally caught a piece of chicken with the sticks and made it to his mouth.

They ate, they kissed, they drank wine. And they laughed a lot. Savanna realized how long it had been since she'd had this much fun. Or this much fun with a guy. She had her friends, but this was different. This was flirty fun.

Somehow, she ended up straddling his lap, the food forgotten. When his hand slipped under her sweater to unhook her bra, she didn't even mind. She knew it was leading there and she was ready. But then he pulled back.

"Do you want to take this to the bedroom?" he asked. "Or am I assuming too much?"

She kissed the edge of his lips. "The bedroom sounds good." He stood, picking her up. She wrapped her legs around his waist. "You know I can walk," she said and giggled.

"Don't ruin this for me. I'm feeling macho." He teased.

"How much wine did you drink?" she asked.

"It's not the wine. It's you." The humor from his eyes faded a touch. "You make me feel good. I haven't felt this good in a long time."

She grinned and a warm gooey feeling filled her chest. "You make me feel good, too." The next thing she knew, he'd laid her on her bed and climbed on top of her.

Chapter Thirteen

She felt so damn right under him. Her arms wrapped around his neck. Their lower bodies fit together and his hips shifted to offer more pressure where he wanted it most. And he wasn't the only one moving. Suddenly, he wanted their clothes gone. He needed to be buried inside her and rocking her to orgasm.

As soon as the thought hit, he realized he needed to slow down. Just because he was already rock hard didn't mean she was ready. Right then, the gentle moves of her body against his stopped. She pulled her mouth from his.

She caught her bottom lip with her teeth. Her brow pinched. "I completely forgot to . . . to get protection. I haven't needed . . . it's been a while."

He leaned on his elbows and smiled. "I bought it." Oh, yeah, he needed to slow down. He wanted to make this good for her.

He brushed a strand of hair from her face. "Do you have any idea how amazingly gorgeous you are?"

She smiled.

He rolled off of her, resting on his side beside her. He picked up a strand of her hair and let it glide through his fingers. "Everything about you is soft." He ran a finger from her hairline to her brow. "A perfect nose." He slid the pad of his finger over her nose, to the cute little cleft on top of her upper lip. "Your mouth invites kisses." He traced the shape of her lips. He slipped his finger inside, then out, and brought it to his lips. "You taste a little sweet. I don't know if it's the hot chocolate, the wine, or just you." He leaned in and kissed her, a quick taste, meant to tease, meant to seduce.

When he pulled back, her eyes were closed. He went back in and kissed her chin this time. He gently turned her head, and ran his finger along the side of her face. "Your ears are tiny, perfectly formed, like a seashell." He traced the delicate shape, then his tongue followed the same path his finger had just traveled.

"I've thought about kissing you here." He pressed a moist kiss right below her ear lobe.

"And here . . ." He moved his lips down the curve of her neck. He slipped his hand under her shirt. Her bra was unhooked and he moved under the soft fabric to find the softer flesh below. "I've thought about kissing you here." He teased her already taut nipple.

Her soft sigh told him he was doing something right. "And I've really thought about kissing you . . ." He ran his finger down her tight abdomen and slowly unsnapped her jeans, unzipped them, then squeezed his hand between the denim and warm skin. "Down here."

She inhaled deeply. His finger moved under the silk of her panties, past the soft patch of hair, and into the cleft of her sex.

This time it was him drawing in a sharp breath. He'd started this to seduce her, but his dick was like wood. And when his finger found her wet, he wanted nothing more than to tear off his jeans and slide into her.

He gently drew his hand out. She moaned a protest. Her eyes were bright, wide and filled with passion. "Don't worry, I'm just getting started." He sat up a bit and pulled off his t-shirt, then he unsnapped his jeans. He reached down and tugged the soft cotton shirt over her head, bringing the bra with it. Her hair fell from the shirt around her bare shoulders.

Her breasts shifted and he leaned down and took one nipple into his mouth.

"That . . . that feels so good," she moaned and slipped her hand around to his back and up to his hair.

"Good." He pulled back savoring the sight of her nipple—wet, rosy and standing erect. "I think the rest of our clothes can go, too, don't you?"

She nodded. Her sweet sexy smile told him she was ready. Shuffling off the bed, he grabbed his wallet, and dropped the two condoms he'd brought on the nightstand. He lowered his jeans and underwear. His dick, hard and ready, bounced against his lower abdomen. He stepped out of his jeans, leaving them there on the floor.

He saw her eyes lower to his sex and widen. She started pulling down her own jeans. "Let me help you." Naked, he crawled back on the bed and straddled her calves. Leaning forward, he grabbed the waist of her jeans. She lifted her bottom and he slowly slid the warm denim down her legs, enjoying the smoothness of her legs as the back of his hands slipped downward. The sight of her sex, right in front of him, had him drawing in another deep breath.

He fit his hands on her waist and slowly let his touch inch lower. He got to the juncture of her thighs and gently spread her legs apart another half inch. He slipped a finger into her sweet dampness.

"You're so wet." He leaned down to kiss her as he slipped his finger inside her. The tight opening surrounded his finger and she let out a throaty sound.

"You like that?" he asked.

"Too much," she said.

"I don't think you can like something too much."

"I think you can," she said, and before he knew what happened, she'd maneuvered him down on the bed and was straddling his legs.

The vision of her naked above him, her thighs slightly parted, her sex open, had his dick throbbing.

She leaned over him, planted her open palms on his chest, then moved in and kissed him. The kiss didn't last long. She rose back up, let her hands slowly glide down his chest, down his abdomen, and she finally took his sex in her hand. She glided her soft palm up and down.

"Okay, you're right," he managed to say. "You can like something too much."

She laughed.

He reached for a shiny package. She took it from him. Using her teeth, she opened it, then rolled the condom down his length.

She leaned down again, lifted her hips. He felt his sex find her soft core, and with a slowness that nearly killed him, she lowered herself on top of him.

When she settled on top of him, he fit his hands around her waist. He rocked her back and forth, and it almost brought him to orgasm.

"Slow or fast?" he asked, barely able to speak.

She started rocking. "Slow," Her pace, an easy movement, was torture. Sweet torture. "And then fast." Her pace increased.

Unable to take it, he rolled her over, and came down on top of her. "Do you mind?"

"Not at all." She offered him another of her precious smiles.

With each push he went deeper. He took it slow at first, and only when he felt her breath catch against his shoulder and felt her tight opening milking him, did he find the pace his body begged for—the fast and hard thrusts that took him over the edge.

• • •

"You . . . okay?" he asked breathlessly.

Savanna couldn't talk, so she nodded against his shoulder.

He came down beside her holding her against his chest. Holding her so close. So tenderly.

"Savanna?"

"Huh?" She managed one word. She'd never considered herself overly educated where sex was concerned. She'd had four different lovers, some better than others, but she'd assumed she'd experienced sex in all its glory.

But the sex she'd known, compared to what she'd just experienced was well . . . like comparing a merry-go-round to a roller coaster. And not a baby roller coaster either, but one that scared the bejiggies out of you.

Never had an orgasm taken her that far. Never had she wanted it so badly.

His little touching and talking foreplay made her ache for more.

Ache to have him inside her.

Ache to make him want her as badly as she wanted him.

Had her aching for more.

She already wanted more.

He brushed her hair from her face. "You okay?"

"Fine."

He studied her. "You sure? You look . . . startled."

"No . . . it was . . . good."

He smiled, and she could swear she noted a little insecurity there. "Just good?"

She grinned. "Amazing."

"That's more like it." He laughed and pulled her against him and rolled over, bringing her on top of him. "But I was thinking more along the lines of phenomenal, or astonishing."

"How about incredible?" she asked.

He kissed her. "I'll take that one, too. Now I'm starved. Let's go finish off the leftovers."

"We just ate."

"No, you ate," he said. "Most of my dinner ended up on my chest."

She giggled. "If you'd let me use a fork, that wouldn't be the case."

"Come on." He stood up, completely comfortable standing there wearing nothing but a used condom. And damn, if he couldn't pull off even that look.

Suddenly realizing she was even more naked than him, she tugged the sheet over her.

"No!" he said. "I worked hard getting you naked, I get to enjoy it for a while longer." He gave the sheet a tug.

She tugged harder.

He fell on the bed and they wrestled, laughing the whole time.

In the end they compromised. She wore his Chinese food-stained t-shirt, but no underwear. He went to the bathroom and donned his boxers.

They ate the rest of the food—well, he mostly ate the food—and they drank the rest of the wine.

Savanna worried he'd refuse to stay the night, and since his house was right across the street, she couldn't even make the point that it was too late to go home. But nope, they sat on the sofa and talked for another hour. He told her more about his travels, and asked her about how she'd decided to open a flower shop. She told him about her favorite vacation as a kid—they'd gone to a dude ranch and her father had gotten skunked. And then he'd stood up, held out his hand, and pulled her back into her bedroom.

He removed her/his t-shirt, saying it had too many stains to sleep in, and then he crawled in bed as naked as she was and made love to her again.

She hadn't believed it could be as good, but she'd been wrong. He'd taken more time. She'd never understood the saying "slow hands" until now. He had the slowest hands, and by the time he got around to touching her where she ached the most, she was almost mad.

As Savanna fell sleep, her head on his chest, she decided it was the best night she'd had in years.

• • •

Mark woke up, Savanna draped on top of him, and he was hard and ready. Her bare breasts rested on his bare chest and it felt nice. He raised his head and noted how her hair scattered around his chest. He smiled. Damn she was pretty and soft and sexy. He recalled how they'd laughed through dinner, how fucking fantastic the sex was. He wanted to kiss her awake, to start making plans for dinner tonight. For more sex. Hell, he wanted to figure out what he needed to buy her for Christmas. When was her birthday? He didn't want to miss her birthday.

His chest gripped.

He needed to get in control of his emotions, this was so new and he was already so . . . invested. But holy hell, how had he gotten here so fast? Logically, statistically, he knew this was probably going to end, and when it did, it was going to hurt like hell.

No! He didn't want to think about it ending.

She lifted her head, her eyes met his.

"Good morning." He smiled. She didn't smile back. "Something wrong?"

"Sorry," she said. "I just . . . It's been a while since I woke up with anyone besides my cat." A meow sounded at her ear.

He watched her tug at the sheet and sit up. She gave her cat a few gentle stokes. He couldn't help but be jealous. He had something for her to stroke, too. Then again, he didn't have a condom. Why hadn't he brought three?

"What time is it?" she asked.

He glanced at her clock. "Five forty-five." Was there enough time to run across the street for a condom? "What time do you have to be at work?"

"I should start getting ready."

Damn.

He could tell she was experiencing a little of the awkward morning-after thing.

"What time do you have to be at work?" she asked.

"Eight."

"You could just stay here and grab another hour of sleep."

It wasn't sleep he was craving. He leaned in and kissed her. "I'll see you tonight. Dinner, right?"

She nodded. "Oh, tonight's Tuesday, I can't. I meet Bethany and Jennifer for dinner every . . . Tuesday."

"Not at Juan's restaurant?"

"No, we're trying that new California Cuisine place on First Street." She bit down on her lip. "I'll be home around eight . . . if you wanted to come over . . . for a glass of wine, or something."

Did something include getting her naked?

"Yeah." He paused and then just said it. "I'll miss you today."

She smiled. "I'll miss you, too."

"How about I make us some coffee while you shower? You do have coffee, right? You have time for a quick cup?"

"Yeah. The coffee's in the fridge. The filters are in the cabinet above the coffee maker."

"Take a shower. I'll have coffee made when you get out. Do you want me to make you some toast or anything?"

"No, I'm fine." She tugged the sheet off the bed and waddled across the bedroom. And looked adorable doing it.

"I saw it all last night," he said. "And a couple of nights before."

She looked back and grinned. "But this is daytime."

"And that makes a difference, why?"

153

Her brow creased. "I don't know, but it does."

He watched her shuffle toward the bathroom and he made himself a promise that he'd get her naked in the middle of the day, just to prove he could. "You're beautiful. You should parade around naked all the time." The door closed then opened and she peered out. "You're not too bad yourself."

"You said I was awesome last night."

He could swear her cheeks flushed with embarrassment. "You were." The door shut. He heard the spray of her shower and he'd give almost anything to join her. To get her all soapy and . . .

He moaned. He'd promised her coffee. He glanced down at his overly optimistic hard-on greeting the day with a big hello.

"Not happening, guy."

• • •

Savanna stepped under the spray of warm water, dropped her chin on her chest and accepted defeat. She'd failed. Failed the have-sex-and-keep-it-casual test.

She knew it the moment he smiled at her right after she'd opened her eyes.

She didn't want to keep it casual.

Oh, she wasn't a fool. She wouldn't go so far to say she loved Mark Donaldson, but the seed felt planted. A seed of possible love. A seed of hope . . . hope for a future. A seed that wasn't at all casual.

Wait, hadn't she done this very thing with Clint? Had sex and then went into planning a lifelong commitment?

Then bam, it hit her all over again. Clint was dead. But for the last eight or nine hours she hadn't even thought about him.

Oh, hell, was that what was going on? Was she fixating on Mark so she wouldn't have to think about Clint? No, that wasn't it. Her heart wasn't that opportunist. The way Mark made her feel, the great sex, the shared laughter, that was . . . real. So real she wanted it to become realer.

But what did Mark want?

I'll miss you today.

She recalled him not wanting to talk about his ex-fiancé. Did he still love her?

He'd also asked if she wanted to slow things down. Perhaps she should have said yes. Taking a deep breath, she decided all she could do was . . . Oh, hell. She didn't have a clue what to do.

Stepping out of the bathroom, the smell of coffee greeted her. Okay, there was something she could do. She could go to work and pretend like she hadn't had the best sex in the world last night. Pretend it didn't matter that Mark was possibly still in love with someone else.

She dressed, did minimal makeup, and then went to start pretending. He was pulling cups down from her cabinet. Shirtless. He looked really good shirtless. She had a few flashbacks of them making love.

Making love?

Why did she look at it as making love? They'd had sex. Get down, get naked, sex.

"Black, right?" he asked.

"Yeah, thanks."

He poured her a cup and brought it to her. She

held it to her lips and stared at him over the rim. The moment grew long.

He exhaled. "Okay, tell me this is just the normal awkward morning-after thing, or do you have re-grets?"

"No regrets. Just maybe a little concern."

"About what?" he asked.

Chapter Fourteen

Savanna hesitated and then just spoke the truth. "That maybe it happened too soon."

He shook his head. "You have to stop thinking like a woman."

She frowned. "I am a woman."

"Oh, I know." His smile came with some sexual innuendo." But you need to stop thinking like one. For a man, it's never too soon. Besides, I've had my eye on you for months."

She arched a brow. "Please. You didn't know I existed until I forced you to—"

"You do lawn work every Sunday afternoon around four. You get home from work at different times, but you have a standing outing most Saturdays around eleven and on Tuesdays you always arrive a little late—like this afternoon."

She grinned, liking that he'd kept up with her. "You're practically a stalker."

He laughed. "Not a stalker. I had you on my radar. Beautiful woman lives across the street, it's natural I would know some things."

"So if you've had me on your radar, why didn't you ever come over and introduce yourself?" Maybe she was wrong about him. Maybe he wasn't still in love with his ex-fiancé. Maybe he was as open to them . . . to them being a "them" as she was.

He picked up his own cup of coffee. "I was worried you lived too close."

She digested that. "And you're not worried about that now?"

He twisted his cup in his hand. "No."

She met his gaze. "Really?"

"I figured it was worth the risk."

Risk? "What risk?" But then she didn't really need to ask. She knew what risk. The risk of what would happen when he told her he really wasn't open to a real relationship. That this was just fun and games. Sex and more sex.

He set his coffee down and stuffed his hands in his jeans. "The risk of . . . You know what, I think what's important is—"

"Don't." She held up her hand. Yup, she should have waited until she knew if he was open to a relationship before she got naked. "I should go to work." Disappointment coiled in her gut. She set her cup in the sink and turned to leave.

"Whoa. No. I didn't mean . . ." He gently caught her by the shoulders and turned her around.

Instantly, she realized she was acting like a psycho girlfriend. They'd spent one night together, and what did she want from him? Promises? What was wrong with her?

"It's okay." She stepped away from his touch.

"It's not okay," he said. "You're obviously upset and I didn't mean—"

"It's not your fault," she said. "I just didn't like that you said there were risks—"

"But I didn't mean—"

"No, you're right. Anytime you meet someone, there are risks. Like with your fiancé. I just . . . I haven't . . . You are the first guy I've seen since my divorce, and I think I'm just . . . mixed up, right now."

"You're not mixed up," he said.

"Yeah, I am. And I think maybe we need to . . . to maybe slow it down."

• • •

Mark dropped down into his office chair.

Jake walked in. "Where's breakfast?"

"Don't start!" Mark didn't look up.

"So dinner didn't go well last night?"

"I said don't start!"

"Alright. " Jake propped his butt against Mark's desk. "I got a call from Mrs. Curley. She's driving home today and said she'd be happy to come talk to us."

Mark looked up. "Can you friggin' please explain how a woman's brain works?"

Jake crossed his arms over his chest. "I'm assuming you don't mean Mrs. Curley?"

"No, I don't mean Mrs. Curley."

"Okay." Jake paused. "Women are . . . difficult. I mean, religion, world politics . . . I could help you out on those, but women . . . they're a mystery."

Mark raked a hand over his face. "I shouldn't have pushed. I knew it was too soon. Her ex-husband was murdered and she's a suspect, her friends are suspects and what the hell do I do but take her to bed? What the hell was I thinking?"

"Shit. You slept with her?"

"I told you not to start!" Mark snapped.

• • •

Savanna was miserable. She'd started to call Mark a dozen times, but to say what? *'I really didn't mean that.'* Jeepers, she was so . . . embarrassed. She'd acted like a fruitcake. He was probably counting his blessings she'd put the brakes on things.

Thankfully, it was a slow day, and since Janice was working, she called an emergency early dinner. At three-thirty, she met her two best friends at the new restaurant. She arrived early, so she walked around the restaurant's little shop.

Her heart clutched when she came across the bins of Jelly Belly jelly beans.

When Jennifer and Bethany arrived, they ordered margaritas, and within a few minutes, Savanna had spilled her guts. She told them about the great sex. About how he made her feel giddy and happy, and how she behaved like a complete idiot.

"It's aftershock," Bethany said.

"I don't think so. The flashes, seeing Clint dead, have stopped."

"Not from Clint's death," Bethany said. "Great sex messes with your mind, especially if you haven't had any in a while."

"She's right," Jennifer said. "Sex can make you stupid."

Savanna moaned. "Why did I do it?"

"Why did you sleep with him, or why did you break up with him?" Jennifer asked.

"I didn't break up with him," Savanna insisted.

Her friends looked at each other and then back at her with their poker faces.

"You think I broke up with him?" Savanna asked.

Bethany put her hand on top of Savanna's. "You sleep with a guy for the first time and then you tell him you need to slow down, that's pretty much a breakup."

"I didn't want to break up with him. What's wrong with me?"

"Nothing," Jennifer said. "You're scared. Clint did you wrong. You lost your mama. Mandy slept with your ex-husband. You've had some tough blows.. It's understandable that you'd be insecure when it comes to building a new relationship."

"Understandable maybe, but still stupid," Savanna said.

"True" Bethany said. "Hey, he's hot. We're not arguing the stupid point."

• • •

Mark and Jake left the retirement home where the witness on a cold case now lived. Mark had just got behind the wheel, when Jake spoke up, "Can I say one thing and then I'll shut up?"

Mark knew what Jake was talking about. "No."

"Good," Jake said. "I've been thinking about what you said about how you were wrong to encourage the relationship because of all the shit happening."

"I said no," Mark growled.

"Yeah, I heard you. I'm ignoring you. You see, when Macy and I met, it was raining shit. I had the crap with my family, and her brother had escaped from prison. There were piles of shit everywhere. But sometimes when crap happens, people need each other. And sometimes when crap happens people do things and say things they shouldn't. If it wasn't for you Macy and I wouldn't be together. What I'm saying is don't give up. Things might work out."

Mark gripped the wheel. "She asked to slow things down."

Jake frowned. "After your first night?"

Mark nodded. "And it's probably best. I didn't have my head completely wrapped around it anyway."

Jake leaned back in the seat. "Because of that Robyn bitch?"

"No." Hell, why was he lying? "Probably. I'm not sure I'm ready for a real relationship."

"Hmm," Jake said. "You think Savanna might have picked up on that and that's why she called it off."

"No," Mark said.

Jake shrugged. "You sure? Women pick up on shit like that. It's like they read you, can see right into our minds. Scares the hell out of me."

Jake's phone rang. He glanced at the screen. "It's Mrs. Curley." He flipped it open. "Jake Baldwin."

Even from the other side of the car, Mark heard Mrs. Curley's panicked voice. "He's dead."

"Who's dead?" Jake looked at Mark.

"Nick. He's dead. He's at my house. He's really, really dead."

"Calm down," Jake said. "My partner and I are on our way."

Mark wasn't sure what 'really, really dead' meant, but he had a few ideas, and he wasn't looking forward to finding out if he was right.

• • •

By the time Mark and Jake pulled up, Piperville's homicide department was already there. Jake's buddy, Tom Hinkle, and his partner stood out front. Mark could guess the reason they were outside was because of the 'really, really dead' comment.

Mark spotted Mrs. Curley and two young boys standing across the street. He had no idea how bad the scene was, but he hoped the young boys hadn't seen it.

Hinkle met them in the middle of the lawn. "She said she called you."

"What we got?" Mark asked.

"You're going to have to see it," Hinkle said. "I'd recommend you cover your nose."

Mark glanced back across the street. "Did the kids go inside?"

"No. Luckily they went over to the neighbor's to get the dog. But the Mrs. didn't get spared."

They walked in the house. The smell was horrendous. Mark's throat tightened. They made their way into the living room.

"Shit!" Mark said.

"I know," Hinkle said. "You're thinking what I'm thinking, aren't you?"

Mr. Curley didn't have a ribbon tied around his dick, but he had one tied around his chest. His throat was slashed, he was naked, and placed under the tree as if he was a gift.

"Yeah," Mark said, but still couldn't see the connection.

"Body's here, it's our case," Tom tossed out the statement.

"I think that's fair," Mark said, the smell turning

his stomach, and making him eager to let go of the case He turned and walked out.

"Totally your case," Jake seconded and followed Mark.

Outside, Mark inhaled trying to clear the smell from his nose.

Mark glanced over at Mrs. Curley. "Can we chat with her?" he asked Hinkle, not wanting to step on anyone's toes.

"I talked to her, but knock yourselves out. If you get something new, however, you let me know."

Hinkle walked back into the house. Mark and Jake went across the street. The first thing they did was get her away from the kids. "Ma'am," Mark started. "I'm sorry for your loss."

Tears filled her eyes. "It's not my loss," she said. "But I feel bad for my kids."

"I'm sure you do," Mark said.

"Ma'am, do you happen to know a Ms. Savanna Edwards, or a Clint Edwards?"

She wiped her eyes. "No. But the other officer asked me that, too. Why?"

Mark inhaled. "I hate to ask hard questions now, Mrs. Curley, but we were told you and your husband had a disagreement a day before he was killed. Do you recall what you were arguing over?"

She hiccupped. "It was . . . he was supposed to be paying my truck payment. And he wasn't. That's why I went to Dallas. To borrow a car from my parents."

Jake and Mark looked at each other. "Was your truck repoed?"

"Yes."

Mark got that ah-haa moment.

"Did you see the man who took your car?" Mark asked.

"Of course. He pulled it right out of my driveway."

"Can you describe him?"

"Hell yeah. Red suit, white beard. It was Santa Claus."

Suddenly, Mrs. Curley paled. "Oh, my God. I told him that all I wanted for Christmas was to have Nick dead and . . . under my tree." She let out a sob. " I didn't mean it."

"We know, ma'am," Jake said.

Mrs. Curley ran to her kids. "Shit," Mark said. "Santa did it. But what doesn't make sense is that Savanna said the only people who heard the ribbon statement were the people at the diner."

"She probably said it to Santa and just doesn't remember."

"I don't think so," Mark said. "I was there most of the time when the wrecker driver was there, and I don't see her saying something like that to anyone but her friends . . . and in a moment of frustration. She's not that crass."

"Maybe Santa followed her to the diner," Jake said.

Mark's gut tightened. "If he did, then maybe he's still following her. She could be in danger." He started the car. If Santa touched Savanna, he was one dead jolly red-suited dude.

Chapter Fifteen

Savanna was in the ladies' room, midstream, when the sound of the main restroom door swishing open filled the small space and she heard a masculine voice call out, "Savanna?"

A masculine voice that sounded a lot like Mark Donaldson. That margarita was stronger than she thought.

She lost her stream. Gave herself a quick pat and dry.

"Savanna?" the voice repeated. Zipping up, certain she was imagining things, she still offered a weak, "Yes."

"You okay?" he asked.

"Yes." Still unsure, she said, "Mark?"

"Yeah."

She stood there a second trying to think. "Why are you in the women's bathroom?"

He didn't answer. When she stepped out of the stall, he wasn't there. Had she imagined it?

When she saw Mark and Jake sitting at the table with her friends, she felt better about her mental status, but still concerned. Why was he here? Her gut said it wasn't about their disagreement. Had they found Clint's killer? They weren't back to thinking it was Jennifer, were they?

When his gaze found hers, she felt an emotional tug on her heart. Had she really broken up with him? Could she take it back?

She moved in and dropped into a chair. "Is something wrong?"

"I think it's time you guys start talking," Bethany said, in her lawyer voice.

Mark met Bethany's gaze. "There's been another murder that appears to be connected to Clint's."

"I've been here all afternoon," Jennifer spoke up. "Ask the waitress." She started trying to flag her down.

"We know." Mark offered her a calm look and then focused on Savanna. "Do you happen to know a Nick or Cindy Curley?" He looked around the table. "Any of you?"

Savanna let the name run around her mind. "No, I don't know anyone by those names."

Jennifer and Bethany both shook their heads.

Jake leaned into the table. "Savanna, when the wrecker driver took your car, did you happen to say anything about your ex?"

She nodded. "I told him the car belonged to me."

Mark spoke up this time. "Did you say anything about wanting him dead with any . . . ribbons?"

Savanna's chest tightened. How many times would she regret saying that? She shook her head. "No, I only said that at the diner. I was mad, and everyone was being silly."

"Could the wrecker driver have followed you there?" Mark asked.

She shook her head. "I don't think so. I mean, I think I'd noticed if Santa Claus was there."

"What if he'd removed the suit?" Mark continued.

"Maybe," Savanna said. And she got the heebie jeebies. "Do you think he's following me?"

"We think it's a possibility," he said.

"No." Bethany broke in. "He wasn't there. I know that for a fact, because I was on the phone with him."

"He was on the phone with you when Savanna said that?" Mark asked and he and Jake looked at each other.

"Yeah."

"Do you think he could have heard her?" Jake asked.

"I . . . I supposed he could have. Shit," Bethany said. "You think Santa Claus did this?"

"Do either of you have the driver's telephone number?" Jake asked.

Bethany pulled out her phone. "I have everything. And he claims his real name is Nicolas Claus. You might be dealing with a crazy."

"He's killed two people," Savanna said. "And you think his name makes him sound crazy?"

"People kill all the time, but they don't change their names to do it." Bethany pushed a few buttons and read off the info. Jake wrote it down. Savanna felt Mark's eyes on her. He was sitting right next to her and she wanted to touch him, but she wasn't sure he'd want that now.

"Thanks." Mark and Jake stood up. His gaze shifted to the others, then back to Savanna. All he did was offer her a nod. What did that mean? Goodbye? Good riddance? Her chest tightened. She watched him start out.

"Don't just sit there, go after him!" Jennifer elbowed her. "He's too hot to let slip through your fingers."

Savanna didn't need to be told twice. She popped to her feet and hurried to the tune of Jingle Bells across the restaurant. The two men had just stepped through the front door.

"Mark?" she called his name as soon as the cold wind hit her face.

He had his hand on the door of his car and he stepped back. Even in the mild, dusky darkness she saw the question in his eyes.

When he stood directly in front of her, she found herself without the right words. "I . . . about this morning, I . . ."

He put a fingertip to her lips. "I understand. You've got a lot of stuff happening right now."

"Yeah, but—"

"I live across the street. We'll talk later." He glanced back at the car where his partner was waiting. "I'm sorry, but we have go and see if we can find this guy."

Her chest gripped. Was his "we'll talk later" an "I'll call you" kind of comment that would never happen?

"Okay." Watching him walk away hurt. Hurt because her gut said what they had, or what they almost had, was gone.

• • •

"Did you apologize?" Jake asked when Mark climbed in the car.

"No. But I told her we'd talk later."

"So there's hope?" Jake asked.

"Yeah," Mark said, "not that it's any of your business."

"The hell it isn't. I already told ya, you're easier to work with when you're getting laid." Jake laughed.

Mark rolled his eyes. But damn if the heaviness

that had settled in his chest since this morning hadn't lightened. He recalled Savanna mentioning something about Robyn and he wondered if Jake couldn't be right. Had he said something that gave Savanna the impression that he wasn't ready to explore what was happening between them?

Hell, maybe he would apologize.

But right now they needed to concentrate on snagging Santa. "So," Mark looked at Jake. "Now do we call your buddy Hinkle and tell him what we got? Or do we chase it down ourselves and take all the glory?"

"Hard call," Jake said. "I do like glory." He frowned. "Hell, let's do the right thing."

• • •

Mark and Jake went back to the precinct and dressed in vests. Considering this guy had killed two people, they decided to take precautions. Mark felt like it was a bit overkill since the weapon of choice from the jolly ol' man was a knife and not a gun. But Jake argued that most wrecker drivers carried guns so Mark conceded. Better safe than sorry.

They met Hinkle and his partner Rodriguez in front of the wrecker service. It was only six-thirty but the night had settled in. A wrecker pulled up right behind them, and the driver got out of his truck. It was Santa.

Jake's phone rang. "We're taking the lead" Hinkle said.

But right then the door to the office opened and out came two men dressed in red suits and wearing beards.

"Ahh, shit!" Jake muttered. "They're all dressed like Santa."

"So we just have to find the real one." Hinkle said.

Mark got out of the car, leery of the Santas in the parking lot.

Jake fell in step beside him. Hinkle and his partner got out of their car and they all walked inside. Two other Santas were in the front office and one stood behind the counter.

"I swear we're not doing anything illegal," one of the Jolly ol' Souls said.

Mark leaned in. "We've got two pick-ups that we think were done by the same guy. A Mustang, belonging to a Clint Edwards, and a truck belonging to a Nick Curley."

"You got dates?" Santa asked and started punching in a few buttons on his computer.

"Clint Edwards was on Saturday the nineteenth. I'm unsure about the other."

He punched a few more buttons. "That would be Nicolas Clausell."

"Is Mr. Clausell working today?"

"He's out on a run." Santa looked Mark up and down. "What did he do?"

"We're just wanting to talk to him," Jake intervened.

"Where's this run at?" Mark asked.

"Off fourth street. You want me to call him?"

"No." Mark leaned in closer. "What's the address to that pick up?"

The man spouted out the address. Jake scratched it down.

"And if he calls, don't mention us, either," Mark

said. "Is he due back here after he picks this one up?"

"Should be, but lately he's been doing some gigs as Santa for some department store across town. He's been written up twice for missing runs."

"Do you have his home address?" Jake asked.

Mark and Jake were going to the place where Mr. Clausell was supposed to be grabbing another vehicle. Hinkle and his partner were going to hang out there and they called for a car to go to Clausell's address in case he went home.

Mar k and Jake pulled up to the address on Fourth Street. Santa was connecting up the car and the owner was giving him hell.

Mark looked at Jake. "You ready?" They both unsnapped their guns.

They got out of their car. Santa glanced back at them and then refocused on the job at hand.

Mark flashed his badge at the car's owner and waved him back. The man must've sensed it was serious, because he did as requested.

Santa must have sensed it was serious, too, because out of the corner of his eye, Mark saw him pull out a gun.

Mark lifted his own weapon out of its holster. "Put it down."

"You put it down," Santa snarled. "Or I'll kill your partner."

Mark cut his gaze to Jake who stood without a weapon in his hand. Mark's heart thumped in his chest.

"Don't use that line," Jake said. "He doesn't even like me that much. I ate his donut this morning.".

"You think this is funny?" Santa asked.

"No, sir," Mark said, his finger on the trigger, his breath in his throat. "No one's laughing. We just want to talk to you."

"You think I don't know why you're here? But what you two don't know is that those men deserved to die. They were no good bums, just like my dad was. They deserved what they got."

"I wouldn't even argue with you on that point," Mark said and eyed the man's hand holding tight to his gun. "Look at me, sir. No one needs to get hurt here."

"Then drop your gun and I'll drive away," Santa said.

Mark ignored that comment and asked, "Is there a Mrs. Clausell? Because if there is, I'll bet she's going to be upset when you get yourself hurt."

"I'm not the one who's gonna be hurt!" Santa growled.

"It's almost Christmas," Mark said. "Do you really want to ruin this season for everyone?"

Santa looked at Mark. At least he wasn't focusing on Jake anymore. But then the Jolly Ol' Soul turned his gun on Mark. Mark fired, but obviously not soon enough. The pain knocked him flat on his back.

Chapter Sixteen

Savanna kept looking out the window to see if Mark was home. He wasn't. His "we'll talk later," obviously hadn't meant tonight. He probably wasn't coming home for fear she'd be waiting. Her heart ached. She felt like crying. Instead, she made her cup of hot chocolate with extra marshmallows and drank it out of the broken cup. She watched Santa lose his pants, and she thought about her mom. Thought about her stupid rule of always, always having a Christmas tree.

She climbed in the attic and pulled down her two-foot artificial tree. The lights were already on it, but she had to hang the ornaments. Ornaments she and her mom had used as a child. She cried a little, and laughed a little remembering all the Christmases of the past.

When the tree was finished, she went to bed, curled up with Boots, and tossed and turned.

Right before midnight she got out of bed and went to look out a window to see if his lights had come on yet. They hadn't. He really didn't want to see her.

She swallowed a hard lump down her throat. Give it up! She went back to bed and laid there staring at the ceiling. She barely knew the guy. She shouldn't feel so depressed.

But she did know him. She knew his childhood of jetting off across the world had been less than perfect. She knew his driver had been more like a parent, and he'd even invested in his restaurant. Yet, Mark still cared enough for his parents that he'd met his mother for coffee. Savanna knew that his favorite candy was an odd flavor of jelly bean, and that he was funny and caring. She knew he was an amazing lover.

That, however, was just the tip of the iceberg. She wanted to know more. She wanted to know it all. She wanted a chance with him.

But she'd ruined that, hadn't she?

In the back of her mind, she heard one of the last things her mother had said to her. "If you want something, Savanna, go get it, don't let anyone stop you."

Tears filled her eyes. She wasn't a quitter. Tomorrow, when she got home from work, she'd go knock on his door. At the very least, he had to give her a chance to apologize for freaking out the way she did. And then . . . then maybe they could try again.

• • •

"You okay?" Jake asked when he walked in and Mark was rubbing his ribs.

"Yeah, just bruised. I told you."

Right then, Logan, one of the night shift homicide cops stuck his head in the door. "You shot Santa Claus. Two days before Christmas and you shot the man. That's priceless."

Mark frowned. "He shot first." Thankfully, he'd had on a vest. But at that close range, he had some seriously bruised ribs.

"I can't wait until the news media gets ahold of this!" Logan said and left.

Mark exhaled. The ribbing from the guys was bad enough, but that was nothing compared to what he'd hear from Washington. Only it wouldn't be in fun. No doubt his dad was pacing and screaming and his mom was already trying to find a way to spin this into a positive piece of media. Then, on her dad's orders, she would call him and give him hell. Remind him who he was, and how important it was to keep the family name clean.

He was so fucking tired of them worrying about the family name. When were they going to start worrying about each other? He thought of his mom, and her seeing a therapist. Was it really going to make a difference?

"Don't let them get to you," Jake said. "I actually know the reason you took that bullet was to get it away from me. Which was stupid, by the way. I was wearing a vest, too, and I was about five feet farther away."

"You would've done the same thing," Mark said.

"No, I'd have shot his merry little ass a lot quicker."

Mark frowned. "You wouldn't have."

Jake grinned.

"Besides," Mark said. "If you'd have taken a bullet and I'd had to tell Macy, she'd have killed me."

"It's good to be loved that much," Jake said with pride. "Speaking of which, I'd better get my ass home. I know she's waiting up on me." Jake rested a hand on Mark's shoulder. "Thanks."

Mark nodded. "Go home to Macy."

Jake walked out. Watching his friend and partner leave, Mark's mind went to Savanna. He didn't know her well enough to start thinking of that kind of relationship, but damn if he wasn't ready to start down that road.

He moved out to the parking lot at a slow pace, his ribs throbbing. Getting in the car hurt like hell. He hadn't stopped moaning when his phone rang. "Hello, Mom," he said not even checking the number.

"How am I supposed to find a positive spin on you shooting Santa?"

Mark was shocked. It wasn't his mom, but his dad. Damn, what had happened? Had his mom stopped taking orders from the old man? Had his mom finally gotten the gall to tell the bastard to go screw himself? Oh, wait, he didn't have to screw himself, he had several mistresses who took care of that.

"How about that I shot him to stop him from shooting my partner, or that I shot him at the same time he shot me!"

"You were shot?" his dad asked, but he didn't sound concerned. More like he thought this might be the spin he needed.

"Yes, but I was wearing a vest, thank you for your concern. Goodnight!" He hung up. He turned his phone off and then headed home.

Fifteen minutes later, when he pulled in his driveway, he looked toward Savanna's. What he wouldn't give to just knock on her door and say, "I'm not sure I can have sex, but I'd love to sleep with you." He was tired of sleeping alone, damnit! He wanted someone at his side. Someone who cared. Someone who gave a damn if he got shot or if he had bruised ribs.

He let go of a deep breath and pulled into his garage. The next time he saw Savanna he needed to tell her he was sorry. They needed to talk. He wasn't sure he had the energy to talk right now.

• • •

Savanna closed the flower shop at noon on Christmas Eve. She ran to the bank, moved some of her mom's life insurance money into her regular account, then hit the streets and did a marathon shopping spree. She dropped five hundred dollars in the Gifts-for-Kids donation bucket. It might be late, but they could always use it for next year.

She got her friends and herself three-day passes to one of the best spas in the Houston area. She got Boots a package of his favorite treats. Then she met Bethany and Jennifer for coffee where they exchanged gifts. Before it got too late, she hurried and bought Mark his Christmas present. Finally, she picked up a few things for herself: a new pair of jeans and red sweater, a pair of red heels, and the sexiest underwear she could find — three sets.

Maybe it was the Christmas magic, but she felt positive. Hopeful. Hopeful she wouldn't be the only one enjoying the underwear.

As she pulled into her driveway around five, she noticed his light on in his living room.

Her hope blossomed more. Okay . . . she needed to do a marathon shower, get dressed in her new outfit and underwear. She could only hope he didn't have plans for the evening. And if he did, she'd do like she'd promised Bethany . . . she'd drive over to her place and spend it with Bethany and her parents. Face it, being alone on Christmas Eve was too sad.

Packages in hand, she placed Mark's gift under the tree. The little tree actually looked better with even one gift under it. She fed Boots, gave him a few strokes and a hug. Then, not wanting to chance Mark leaving, she ran into the shower.

Ten minutes later, only wearing underwear and some makeup, she heard her doorbell.

Her heart did a tumble. Could it be him? Haphazardly tying on her pink nubby robe, she tore off for the door.

Remembering to look through the peephole first, she got up on her tiptoes and glanced out. It was him. Him, looking all wonderful.

She yanked open the door, a big smile on her face. "Hey," she said, noticing he held two gifts in his hands.

"Hi." He smiled. "You look as if you're getting ready to go somewhere."

"I was," she said.

"Oh, well, I just wanted to give you . . ."

"I was hoping to spend the evening with my neighbor."

His eyes widened and so did his smile. "Really?"

"Yeah, well, if he didn't have any plans." She stepped back. "Wanna come in?"

"Love to." His eyes lowered and she knew her robe had probably come open and given him a peek at the red and black bra.

His gaze went to the twinkling tree on the table against the wall. "You put up a Christmas tree."

She sighed. "My mom loved Christmas. She would have turned over in her grave if I hadn't."

He smiled. "Can I put these there?"

She watched him set the gifts on the table. "That's your gift," she said.

He turned around. "You got me a gift?"

She nodded. "Don't act surprised. I'm assuming those are for me. Or am I wrong?"

He grinned. "They're for you. But only one's from me. The other is . . . from my mom."

Savanna's mouth dropped open. "Your mom got me something for Christmas?"

"Yeah, surprised the hell out of me, too." He walked over and brushed a strand of hair behind her ear. "We need to talk."

A little tremble of fear stirred in her gut. Was he going to tell her he didn't want a real relationship?

She nodded. "I hope it's good."

"I . . . I need to say I'm sorry if I gave you the wrong impression . . ."

Oh, shit. Here it came. He was just a guy looking for a good time. Her heart gripped. "It's about your ex-fiancé, isn't it?"

"No! I mean, yeah, sort of. The thing is, if I led you to believe that there's something still between us, there isn't. I won't lie. I've stayed away from anything serious since then. Hell, I'll even admit that this . . . this thing between us scares me, but . . ."

"I'm scared, too," she blurted out, "That's why I acted like an idiot. I don't want to slow this down, I want . . . to move forward."

He moved closer, wrapped his hand around her waist. "Forward sounds good."

He kissed her. A soft, sweet sexy kiss. When he pulled back, her robe had come loose and he arched a brow at her underwear.

"Nice." He smiled with interest.

"It's a gift," she said.

"For me?" he asked in his sexy tone.

"No, for myself. But I don't mind sharing." She opened her housecoat and gave him a quick peek of the matching panties.

"Wow, I'm worried my gift isn't going to hold a candle to this." He ran a finger down the black bra strap.

"I want you to open my gift to you." She closed her robe and went and got his gift. "Here."

He took it. "Okay, but first open the one my mom sent. "I'm curious to what . . . I haven't a clue what got in her head. And if it's bad, I apologize in advance."

Savanna reached for one of the gifts. "No, it's the smaller one." She picked up the package. It was light. She tore back the paper. She opened it up and found a note.

So you don't have to wear my son's.

She laughed and read him the note. "I was wearing your robe when she knocked on the door." She pulled out the black silk fabric and found a beautiful robe. "I think I might learn to like your mom," she said.

"Don't push it," he said.

She dropped her pink nubby robe and donned the silk one. "It even matches my underwear."

"That it does, but you really don't need to wear it," he said, a sexy twinkle in his eye.

"Now open yours," she said.

"I'd rather open your gift." He raised an eyebrow and swept his gaze over the lingerie she was wearing.

"Open it," she insisted and held the box out to him.

He opened it and pulled out the cup. When he saw what was in it, he grinned. "Tell me these are Chili

Mango Jelly Bellies, and I'll love you forever."

It was the word 'love' that had her smiling the biggest. She wasn't sure how it had happened, but she was there, right at the edge of falling.

"Where did you get them?" he asked. "I usually have to order them."

She watched him open the bag and pop a jelly bean into his mouth. "Here, try this and tell me it's not heaven." He put one in her mouth.

She savored the spicy sweet flavor. "It's good."

"No, it's great!" he told her. "Really, where did you get these?"

"They sell them in that Everything California restaurant in their gift shop."

He looked at the cup that held the bag of candy. "And I get a Jelly Belly mug. How cool is that?" He moved in and kissed her again.

"Thank you," he said. "Now open my gift." He set his present down in a chair and brought her the other one. "Although, I think my mother probably outshined me." He popped another jelly bean into his mouth.

"I'm sure it's perfect." She sat down on the sofa and glanced up at him. What was perfect was him being here. What was perfect was that she wasn't alone on Christmas Eve.

"Open it," he said.

The present was in a big square box and heavy. "What could this be?" She gave it a slight shake.

"It's breakable," he warned.

She ripped off the paper. The cardboard box didn't have any writing on it, so she opened it. And when she saw what it was, tears filled her eyes. She pulled the first one out and saw it was the heat activated cup where Santa lost his pants. A few tears slipped down her lashes.

"There's a set of four cups. They're slightly different ones," he said and then he looked at her face. "Okay, tell me it's not so bad that I made you cry? I thought you collected them. You asked about where I got that one and I thought—"

"No." She wiped her cheeks. "You don't understand. Mom and I exchanged Christmas cups every year. This . . ." She held up the cup she'd pulled out. "This was the last one she gave me and I accidentally broke it." Her voice shook.

She set the cups down and moved to hug him. "I didn't think I'd ever get another mug for Christmas."

"So I didn't screw up?" he asked, folding his arms around her.

"No, you couldn't have given me anything more perfect." She leaned in and whispered the words right before she kissed him. "Merry Christmas."

The kiss lasted and lingered. He untied the silk robe. "Can I unwrap your gifts now?" He looked down at the matching underwear outfit. "We might have to take it a little easy, though."

"Easy?" she asked.

"I'm guessing you didn't see the news?"

"What news?" she asked.

"The media has dubbed me the cop who stole Christmas. I shot Santa. But only after he shot me."

"You were shot?" She started running her hands over his chest. "Where?"

"I was wearing a vest, but it bruised the hell out of my ribs."

She started unbuttoning his shirt. When she saw the ugly purple mark she frowned. "That looks painful." She barely touched the side of the bruise.

He looked down at her and smiled. "Personally, I think you just wanted to get my shirt off."

"Maybe." She grinned and then frowned back at his mark.

He pulled her against him again. She made sure not to lean against his right side. "Thank you," he said.

"For what?" she asked.

"For being here. For caring." His hand moved her back, tenderly caressing her. "For spending Christmas eve with me. And Christmas day," he said. "I'm hoping you're open."

"There's no other place I'd rather be," she said.

He leaned down and kissed her. "Yup. I like this moving forward thing."

"Me, too," she said. "Me, too."

More Sexy, Suspenseful and Seriously Funny Books by Christie Craig . . .

Divorced, Desperate and Delicious

"Christie Craig delivers humor, heat, and suspense in addictive doses. She's the newest addition to my list of have-to-read authors . . . Funny, hot, and suspenseful. Christie Craig's writing has it all. Warning: definitely addictive."

— *New York Times* bestselling author Nina Bangs

After photographer Lacy Maguire caught her ex playing Pin the Secretary to the Elevator Wall, she's been content with her dog Fabio, her three cats, and a vow of chastity. But all that changes when the reindeer-antlered Fabio drags in a very desperate, on-the-run detective who decides to take refuge in her house.

Divorced, Desperate and Dating

"This sequel to Craig's *Divorced, Desperate and Delicious* is another delightfully entertaining novel with an intriguing mystery. Peopled with interesting new characters and familiar old ones, it also has its share of animal friends that add a lot of humor and warmth to the story."

— *RT Book Reviews*

Mystery writer Sue Finley had given up on real men and was sticking to the ones she could kill off in her books, but when she starts receiving death threats, she'll have to rely on Detective Jason Dodd to be her real-life hero.

Divorced, Desperate and Deceived

"The fun — and action — never stops in the enchanting *Divorced, Desperate and Deceived*. Christie Craig's prose practically sparkles with liveliness and charm in the exciting conclusion to her stunning *Divorced, Desperate and Delicious* Club trilogy."

— Joyfully Reviewed

Kathy Callahan, the last "surviving" member of the Divorced, Desperate & Delicious club, wouldn't let herself get trapped in another relationship like her friends did. But maybe a simple dalliance with her sexy, hot plumber wouldn't be such a bad thing. Trouble is, the guy snaking her drain is an undercover cop, handier with a gun than a wrench, and life just got a whole lot more complicated.

Weddings Can Be Murder

"Ms. Craig delivers a well-paced and well-plotted mystery that will keep you guessing to the last page without compromising the happily-ever-after romantic ending."

— Fresh Fiction

Katie Ray was about to marry a man she didn't love—and who didn't love her. Even losing her $8,000 engagement ring wasn't enough of a sign to call things off. What did it take? Being locked in the closet with a sexy PI, and being witness to murder.

Gotcha!

"The mystery and romance plots fit seamlessly into a witty and fast-paced novel that's easy to read and satisfying to the heart."

—Publishers Weekly

The men in Macy Tucker's life have always been undependable, including her foolhardy brother who just escaped from prison. The investigating detective, Jake Baldwin, is proud, inflexible . . . and very, very sexy. Whether she likes it or not, she'll have to trust him with her life and maybe even her heart.

Shut up and Kiss Me

"Quirky, touching and fun!"
   —New York Times bestselling author Susan Andersen

Photojournalist Shala Winters already had her hands full bringing tourism to this backward, podunk town, but her job just got tougher. Pictures can say a thousand words, and one of Shala's is screaming bloody murder. Now she has to entrust a macho, infuriating lawman with her life—but she'll never trust him with her heart.

Murder, Mayhem and Mama

Cali lost her mom to cancer. Detective Brit Lowell lost his partner to murder. Now he's in the mood to take down some dirtbags, and Cali's ex just happens to be a dirtbag, leaving a trail of dead bodies behind him. Can Brit trust this beautiful woman to help take down her ex? Can Cali look past this sexy cop's hard exterior to trust him with her heart? Can life get any crazier when Mama's spirit starts meddling from the grave?

The Hotter in Texas Series . . .

"Hold on to your Stetsons . . . A thrill ride of hunky heroes, high jinks, and heartwarming romance."
— *New York Times* bestselling author Lori Wilde

Only in Texas

Nikki Hunt thought her night couldn't get worse when her no-good, cheating ex ditched her at dinner, sticking her with the bill. Then she found his body stuffed in the trunk of her car. Former cop turned PI Dallas O'Connor knows what it's like to be unjustly accused. But one look at the sexy—though skittish—suspect tells him she couldn't hurt anyone, and he'll do all the undercover work he has to in order to prove it.

Blame It on Texas

Zoe Adams' life turns into an episode of one of the unsolved mystery shows she loves to watch on TV, when she realizes she may be a long-lost heiress, kidnapped as a baby from a wealthy Texas family. PI Tyler Lopez realizes Zoe's story is just crazy enough to be true, and when the bullets start flying he becomes determined to never let her be a victim again.

Texas Hold 'Em
(coming January 2014)

The last thing veterinarian Leah Reece needs is a man in her life. They're nothing but trouble—and not even the fun kind. But when her apartment is broken into and Leah suspects Rafael, her dangerous half brother, of foul play, she can't deny she could use a little help. She just never expected that help would come with twinkling blue eyes and a sexy smile . . .

And the **New York Times** *Bestselling*
Shadow Falls Series
writing as C. C. Hunter . . .

Born at Midnight
Awake at Dawn
Taken at Dusk
Whispers at Moonrise
Chosen at Nightfall
Turned at Dark (novella)
Saved at Sunrise (novella)

One night Kylie Galen finds herself at the wrong party, with the wrong people, and it changes her life forever. Her mother ships her off to Shadow Falls—a camp for troubled teens, but it soon becomes clear that the kids at Shadow Falls are far from ordinary. They're supernatural—learning to harness their powers, control their magic and live in the normal world. Kylie's never felt normal, but surely she doesn't belong here with a bunch of paranormal freaks either. Or does she?

About the Author

New York Times bestselling author Christie Craig grew up in Alabama, where she caught lightning bugs, ran barefoot, and regularly rescued potential princes, in the form of bullfrogs, from her brothers. Today, she's still fascinated with lightning bugs, mostly wears shoes, but has turned her focus to rescuing mammals and hasn't kissed a frog in years. She now lives in Texas with her four rescued cats, one dog—who has a bad habit of eating furniture, a son, and a prince of a husband who swears he's not, and never was, a frog.

If Christie isn't writing, she's reading, sipping wine, or just enjoying laughter with her friends and family. As a freelance writer, Christie has over 3,000 national credits, as well as three works of non-fiction, including the humorous self-help/relationship book, *Wild, Wicked & Wanton: 101 Ways to Love Like You're in a Romance Novel*. Christie writes humorous romances novels for Grand Central, as well as the *New York Times*-bestselling Shadow Falls series, under the pen name C.C. Hunter. Contact Christie—she loves hearing from readers—or learn more about her and her work through her website: www.christie-craig.com